THE FACE OF DEATH

The *hougan*'s voice continued hypnotically repeating his message. The people's eyes were on him and on the snake, now draped partly over the platform's edge. Then the din ceased abruptly.

In the silence, Balthazar heard the thud of horse's hooves in the sand. Heads turned toward the sound. Those on the far edges began shrieking.

In the moonlight, a white horse was running wildly, the figure on its back indistinct. There was an upright stick in the rider's hand, looking like a raised sword. The horse plunged toward the tightly packed crowd, and people leapt, scrambling madly out of its way. The rider slid off, but the horse ran forward still.

The crowd, first bent on getting out of the way of the horse's flailing hooves, was now just as frantically avoiding the man. There were a few cries of "zombi!" But most drew back in horrified silence. The newcomer lurched forward beneath the sickly yellow spotlights onto the wooden floor of the restaurant, supporting himself with the stick.

Balthazar himself could do nothing but stare. The man had only half a face. . . .

Bantam Books offers the finest in classic and modern American murder mysteries. Ask your bookseller for the books you have missed.

A
FEBRUARY
FACE

M. J. Adamson

BANTAM BOOKS
TORONTO • NEW YORK • SYDNEY • AUCKLAND

A FEBRUARY FACE
A Bantam Book / April 1987

ISBN 0-553-26540-7

Published simultaneously in the United States and Canada

Bantam Books are published by Bantam Books, Inc. Its trademark, consisting of the
words "Bantam Books" and the portrayal of a rooster, is Registered in U.S. Patent and
Trademark Office and in other countries. Marca Registrada. Bantam Books, Inc., 666
Fifth Avenue, New York, New York 10103.

PRINTED IN THE UNITED STATES OF AMERICA

O   0 9 8 7 6 5 4 3 2 1

In memory of R. S. Shannon, Jr.

DON PEDRO: . . . Why, what's the matter
That you have such a February face,
So full of frost, of storm, and cloudiness?
Much Ado About Nothing

ACKNOWLEDGMENTS

Again, my thanks to members of the San Juan Police Department, and especially to Ed Poullet of the Community Relations branch. I am grateful to Dr. Elspeth MacHattie for her thorough reading.

AUTHOR'S NOTE

Knowledgeable readers will be aware that throughout this book I have used Haitian terms for the system of beliefs generally called Voodoo. In Puerto Rico, the term for these traditional African practices is *santeria*, and the spirits, although very similar in conception, have different names. However, because most readers are more familiar with Haitian forms, I adopted these. Given the private ceremonies I occasionally glimpsed in Puerto Rico's rain forest, the rites seem very close to those I described. There is, of course, an actual Loiza Town, whose history and beautiful setting I hope I accurately portrayed. Their festival in honor of Saint James is justly famous, they do make wonderful devils' masks, and at certain seasons, dead chickens festoon the telephone wires. The townspeople would probably not be at all surprised at the occurrences I have only imagined.

1

LORENA GARCIA WAS badly frightened. She told herself that she had never been so frightened in her life.

Although she was a woman given to exaggeration, this was true. Her whole body trembled with the cold ague of fear. If she had unclenched her teeth, they would have shaken themselves loose. Her eyes were squinched together so tightly that they disappeared into her round black cheeks.

But she had to open them occasionally for a quick desperate glance down the beach to see if the young man was returning yet.

Why didn't he come? The nearest phone was a long way away but it seemed to Lorena that she had been waiting for a very long time.

She had to look over her shoulder to make sure that the body was still lying on the edge of the water and not walking with slow, dragging steps toward her.

She made herself look at it again.

The corpse was that of a relatively young black man, powerfully built. His eyes had sunk into his face, and the face had spread out as if the bones had started to melt, causing the mouth to turn down slightly in a malignant frown. In the forehead, there was a small black hole with raw, burned edges.

Lorena had seen dead men before. Not just embalmed bodies, either. But they were dead people she knew, and she had been surrounded by other people at the time.

This body, although Lorena didn't know it, was in fact embalmed.

Had she known it, though, it would have made no difference. *Zombis* could be embalmed and still get up and walk again, she was sure. They had to be killed *twice* and she had no way of knowing in this case.

She swore to herself that she would never come out again before dawn to get sticks of wood for the fire. Always, from now on, she would do it the day before. At noon. But she *had* wanted her coffee.

And never, never again would she neglect the Voodoo spirits. She would always leave food for them. She would talk to the really old people of Loiza and find out everything that must be done. They would remember even though most people in Puerto Rico paid no attention to the necessary rites.

Everyone believed in the spirits, of course, but they called them by Spanish names. Somehow these renamed spirits didn't seem as powerful to Lorena. Nor as threatening. And not since she was young had she heard anyone mention *zombis*.

This was at least the fourth *zombi* in the last few months. The *loa*, the Voodoo spirits, were no longer willing to protect the forgetful people of Loiza.

Everybody had been talking about it, in every little roadside bar in the town. But they kept hoping it had nothing to do with them. They would have another rum or beer and try to forget it. But now she knew. She would talk to Junior Pabon, and to Momée. Now, they would have to do something.

She opened her eyes and still, all along the lonely stretch of beach, there was no sign of the young man.

At first, when she emerged from the trees, the body had been covered with water and she had only seen the head, bobbing up and down. Thinking it was a coconut, she had gone to retrieve it. Only then could she see the whole body, waving its arms and legs in the tide.

She had screamed and screamed. When the young

jogger reached her and grabbed her to make her stop, his rough touch had almost driven her out of her wits.

He had pulled the horrible thing farther up on the sand. He told her to stay while he went to call the police.

If she had been able to think, Lorena would have told *him* to stay there while she left. But she was rather fat and no longer young. The young man was clearly a fast runner.

And there was no hope that she could just leave and hurry back to her own tiny house and bolt the door. That would just induce the *zombi* to follow her. He would know where she lived. He would come at night when she was alone in the dark.

So she stayed, desperately clutching the square of embroidered cloth that her old friend Junior Pabon had "arranged" for her. It was attached to her bra, along with a silver medal of Saint James, with a rusty safety pin. Junior had sworn that this would keep all evil away and surely he must know because his father was a *hougan*, a Voodoo master, years and years ago, when she was young.

Then everyone in the little rural town, every black, had gone to the Voodoo ceremonies.

She had been afraid then, too, but that had been a delicious campfire fear. Her mother was there. And there was good food to eat, which was important in those days before the government of the United States starting sending checks, because sometimes the people had nothing to still their hunger but watered coconut milk.

The ceremonies were festive occasions. The drum beat was irresistible. Flames from huge bonfires lit the dark night, and there were little candles everywhere around the edges of the *hounfor*. The large, open structure with its roof of palm fronds stood in the middle of a field. Charms hung everywhere from the roof and from the thin poles that held it up. There were scarves and flags and painted coconut shells. The center pole was decorated especially for Damballah, the snake, in case he appeared in his own form and wanted to slither down.

Lorena struggled to remember if he ever had. Usually, she remembered, he possessed one of the adults. Then that person would fall into a fit, roll on the ground in convulsions, then, although still trembling, rise and speak to the others with a hiss. The people would be told of past and future events.

Sometime other spirits came and possessed people. The Guédé, the spirits of the dead, were jokers, and when someone was possessed by one of them, he lifted the dresses of the women and felt their breasts and talked about what they had been doing that they shouldn't. Sometimes they possessed a woman and made her do naughty things to the men. But everyone laughed. They were funny. And you had to be very, very careful with the Guédé.

And most careful of all of Baron Samedi, the master of the dead. But he rarely came and possessed anyone.

Maybe if she stood there on the silent, empty beach and thought about the spirits, they would protect her from the *zombi* and the sorcerer who had sent him. She muttered a heartfelt prayer to Saint James. He could come riding down the beach on his horse and save her. But no, he was a saint, not a spirit.

When she was young, she always got mixed up. The priest said while there were definitely saints, there were no *loa*. But he was wrong. Everyone knew there were *loa*. How else could you explain the way things happened to some people? Take care of the *loa* and good things fall in your lap. You become rich. If you became sick, and the doctors, even the doctors in San Juan, couldn't help you, you got better anyway.

But when the *loa* were angry, they no longer protected you from all the really dreadful things. When she'd left the ceremony in the old days, she'd cling to her mother's side going home in the dark. Both of them watched carefully for the columns of people walking silently through the night. Many of the townsfolk had seen them. If they saw you, they asked you questions.

If the *loa* didn't put the right answers in your head, you had to join the column.

And there were strange animals. Junior's father said one night a large dog with yellow eyes jumped out of a clump of pine trees near the beach and lunged at him. The *hougan* hit and hit it with a stick, but still it snarled and tried to spring at him. Finally, he grasped a vial of "arranged" water and threw it in the dog's face. Instantly, standing before him was the Chief of Police from the next town. His face and shoulders were covered with marks from the stick, and he begged the *hougan* not to tell and slunk off into the night.

The police. Could she even trust them when they came? Even Sergeant Terron, whom she'd known from his boyhood? Would he know how to handle a *zombi*?

Why didn't the young man hurry? But, of course, he didn't know, didn't really understand, even though he'd probably been born in Loiza.

All the older people knew that *zombis* were the worst. A sorcerer had passed a bottle under the dead person's nose and captured his soul, and from then on, the *zombi* must do all he was told. Always in the past, people had taken preventive measures. When someone died, you strangled them or shot them in the head right away. And, of course, sewed up their mouths, because a corpse could only be raised if it answered its name. You had to make sure that the corpses had enough to do in the grave. When her mother had died, they put an eyeless needle in the coffin so she would keep trying and trying to thread it.

But once someone was turned into a *zombi*, there was nothing you could do to protect yourself from him.

Trembling, she looked at the body near her.

It was back in the water.

It was moving.

It was trying to roll over on its knees and get to its feet.

She fell over in a dead faint. She didn't see the young jogger rushing back up the beach toward her.

2

MOMÉE MOLINA SLIPPED her needle carefully through the corpse's lips as she worried aloud to her companion, a wiry old black man who stood beside her in the unsteady light of the candles. Although the flesh on the woman's upper arms hung loosely, quivering as she worked, it was evident that in her late sixties she was still strong and vigorous.

"We are being punished, Junior. We have not done the right thing for many, many years."

Junior, a little older and much grayer than Momée Molina, did not reply. He handed her some cotton wool from the assortment of items they had spread on the table next to the body. The room was lit only by the short fat candles, but above them were long rows of fluorescent lights.

The frail, almost skeletal corpse lay on a modern embalming table, and the walls were lined with white-painted steel cabinets. At one end of the room there were two tall refrigerators and an enormous stainless steel sink. At the other end were a large gray desk and two upright chairs. The newness—and the sterility—of the room and its contents contrasted sharply with the bits of feathers, string, small pots, and brilliantly decorated rattle the old couple were using.

Seeing the woman was almost finished with the body's mouth, Junior picked up the bright, bead-encrusted rattle and began muttering under his breath. He pointed the rattle to all four directions, starting with the East, and alternately sang an unintelligible song and chanted Catholic prayers.

"There," he said finally. "I have asked the help of the Water spirit, the *loa* Agwa, just as I was taught."

She stopped sewing and stared at him in horror.

"You did not say his name correctly! It is Agwé. Agwé-taroyo. He will be angry. He will keep putting the dead on the beach!" Ashen-faced, she sat down abruptly, leaving the needle dangling from the mouth of the dead man.

"If only old Luis had not died," she wailed. "He would have been able to tell us how these things are done exactly. He was ninety, always forgetting everything, but he remembered all the rituals. What are we to do?" She crossed her arms across her large breasts and rubbed her shoulders slowly.

The old man was crestfallen and more than a little frightened, but he moved to the end of the room to comfort her.

"Momée, is true that these last years we have not followed the rites as we should. The *loa* may be hungry. We have not put out food. And they might, too, be starved for news. But here in Loiza, and nowhere else, I think, in Puerto Rico, we have kept all the powerful Voodoo materials—the three kinds of drums, the scarves, the pitchers, the rattles, the bowls. And also, we go to church when we should. We take communion. The saints will tell the *loa* that they see us, that we mean well."

"Could be." She shivered and dropped her voice to a whisper. "We will take all the money that the funeral director, Señor Coret, gives us for our help here and take it to Father Gutierrez for Masses for the Dead. And I myself have not neglected Agwé, since I live much nearer the beach than you. Always at the full moon, I put out food for him. The white food the water spirits like. It's not the same food he used to get at the great ceremonies—bananas fried in sugar, breast of chicken, mangoes, white rum. But I do what I can. I lay out a little rice in milk, fried egg, and sometimes

7-Up. I had thought of Coca-Cola, he might like that better, but 7-Up is the right color, so that's why I thought I'd better . . ." She moved again to the corpse, cutting the thread from the lips after knotting it. She stuffed more cotton wool in the nostrils and a great deal in the ears.

"There, now I have closed up his ears, but we should still speak very low, I think." She gestured toward the corpse. "He might carry messages to the other dead, even . . ." her whisper was barely audible, "to Baron Samedi."

The old man glanced around the room worriedly.

"But we should have done more. I feel it, Junior." She pronounced the name with the Spanish *h* for *j*, and the name seemed an odd choice for the stooped, gap-toothed old man. But she knew that, out of his respect for his well-known father, the old man had not taken his father's and his own name, as the many Puerto Rican sons called Junior do after the death of the parent.

"When your father left the living, you became *hougan*. I have been *mambo* for thirty years. We should have held more ceremonies, taught the young. It was our duty."

Frowning, she picked up a wide strip of cloth from the table and, slipping it under the chin of the corpse, swiftly tied the two ends in a knot on the top of the dead man's head. Selecting a thinner strip, she moved to the end of the table and firmly tied the big toes together.

"So," she went on, "perhaps we deserve this terrible problem. These bodies. It is now February. I think there have been five left on the beach since October. People in town say there may have been many, many more. They say that now when the *Policía* find them, they take them away immediately. Right away. They no tell us."

The old man lowered his voice. "Have *you* seen any of them yourself? Are they *zombis*?" He glanced fearfully around the room as if making sure there were none about.

"No, no, I have not seen them. Lorena Garcia, she say she has, and old Julio, too. I ask them both a lot of questions. But who can believe Lorena—she makes up such stories! And old Julio, one is never sure he understands. But when Señor Coret comes to ask our help, I ask him what he knows. He say the bodies were all already dead before they were put on the beach. But he say they were all shot in the head later, after they died. He say he does not know where they come from, that no one knows. Our cemetery has not been dug up. But it is always well-locked."

"But are they *zombis*?" the old man persisted.

"How could Señor Coret know that?" she asked impatiently. "He is only a young man—only forty-five or so. And these bodies, they are found always by even younger men, too, jogging on the beach early in the morning." She said 'jogging' with a heavy Spanish *h* sound in the beginning of the word. "But you and I, we couldn't have told by then. If we had seen them walking around before they were killed the second time, we would have known. . . ."

"So my father would have said," the man replied slowly. "He say that when a sorcerer calls a dead one from the grave, he can order the dead man to do anything. Work him very, very hard. Feed him almost nothing. Beat him. As long as he gives the dead no salt, the sorcerer can keep him forever as a slave. You can tell that he is a dead, my father say, by the way he acts. A *zombi* moves slow, looks around funny like he doesn't know where he is, doesn't move his eyes, talks through his nose. The *zombi* must do all he is told. Even evil things."

"*Sí*, and this is what I think. One of two things. A powerful sorcerer is calling the dead forth to do evil. Then he kills them again and sends them back. Or it could be the *loa* who have sent the dead to us to remind us of our duties."

"But *which loa*?" the old man wailed plaintively. "At Christmas, we sacrificed many, many chickens. We hung them on all the telephone wires where the roads come into Loiza. Bad luck should have stayed away. There have been two more bodies since then. Maybe it's not Agwé." He pronounced it carefully, making the sign of the cross as he did so.

"Perhaps, Damballah, the Snake?" The old woman removed her turban and scratched her head thoughtfully. "You know, Junior, he also is of the water spirits."

"Damballah, perhaps." The old man thought. "He lives in the rivers and the swamps. These bodies have been found near the ocean, is true, but between the two rivers, where they go into the sea. Damballah might like it if we older ones all took a pilgrimage. Up the *Espiritu Santo* River right to the rain forest. We could hire a bus. Have a ceremony at the foot of the mountain, *El Yunque*. We have not had a pilgrimage for a long time. And everyone enjoys them."

"It is an idea, Junior. We could bring much food and use one of the little huts in the picnic area back in the forest for a temporary *hounfor*. All the older people would remember Damballah. They would come."

"*Sí*, and," the old man added craftily, "we could include our charge in the price of the bus."

"But you know," and here even the woman glanced around in some trepidation, "it could be Baron Samedi, Master of the Cemetery and of the Dead. He must give his approval before the dead are sent."

"Momée, this is *different*. These bodies—that is not the same thing at all as 'sending dead.' When dead are sent, their bodies no come. Just their souls. And they enter into the living and make them sick. The living man who has been entered by the dead becomes very ill, very thin, spits blood." He quickly turned to the corpse, "You don't think," he stuttered, "that old man was. . . ."

"No," the woman said firmly, trying to sound assured. "He die of hole in the stomach. I know his wife. She say it was too much rum. But it is hard to know what to do, Junior."

She walked to the far end of the room again and slumped wearily into the chair.

"These ceremonies cost money. If we have one for all the possible *loa* and still the bodies come . . . well, the people will think we are not good. That the *loa* no come to us when we call them. Then we will get no money at all for any services."

The old man looked dismayed. He counted on the small fees he was paid to "arrange" various charms that kept away evil. Suddenly he sat up.

"But if we tell the people this problem needs the help of a very experienced *hougan*, someone who is used to dealing with such great evil—let him solve it. Then if it no works, it is *his* fault."

"But," the woman objected, "there is no one on this island—"

"From Haiti," the old man said triumphantly.

"We would have to bring him here and give him much money," the woman mused.

"Is no so far, next island over," the man said. His thin face was alight with new hope. "And not so much money for him either. They are very poor in Haiti. We ask for some money from each of the older people. And we ask them on government check day."

"We don't know any names of *hougan* in Haiti, though, Junior."

"Maybe we ask Señor Malen. His mother, she believed strongly in Voodoo when she lived. He grew up in Mameyes, near here, near the rain forest. And he had a factory in Haiti when he lived in New York. He might know."

"He will call us superstitious, think we are stupid blacks," the old woman objected. "He is a rich man now—lived in New York for thirty years."

"*Sí, sí*, but he may tell us. Out of respect for his mother. But . . . maybe we just ask Señor Malen for the money to pay. He will give us some if we tell him it is for the old people of the town. We ask the people here with relatives in the Dominican Republic to find a *hougan*. They could find out."

"We should do it soon, Junior. February has not a

good soul. Dangerous—although no so bad a time of year as Christmas."

The old man suddenly struck his thigh angrily. "How can we talk to this man from Haiti? They do not speak Spanish there. French, or something."

"True, who would speak both French and Spanish?" They looked at each other in despair.

"The two *Norteamericanos*, Junior," Momée said, snapping her fingers. "The ones who come every winter to live on the beach. In *Playa del Mar*. They speak Spanish now. No at first. But now. And she writes books, they say. She will also then speak French."

"*Sí*," the old man said, looking at her, "the large man with the bald head like a coconut. He is nice, smiles always, very strong. He help me with the wood from the beach. He say he like my hat, needs one like mine to keep sun from his head. . . . But, no. Then they would both know what we do. We would have to tell her so she could tell the man from Haiti. And some say those *Americanos* are *gobierno*. Not *gobierno de* Puerto Rico. The government of *Los Estados Unidos*. Maybe we should not let *gobiernos* know what we do."

"Why?" Momée Molina was clearly reluctant to give up the idea. She had always wanted to talk to that couple, to see what the inside of the house looked like. She could then describe it, imply that they were friends of hers.

"Maybe the checks will not come if the government knows about the Voodoo."

"Why should they care?" the mambo returned, although it was clear that she was shaken. There were many old people in Loiza and they all depended on the checks.

There was a quiet knock on the door.

"It is Señor Coret," the man whispered. "We will think more tomorrow."

He rose and opened the door. "Please come, Señor. We have finished. There are, of course, a few further directions," the old man said importantly.

The funeral director, a slim, attractive man in his

early forties, looked at the body in some bemusement. "Why have you tied up the head so?"

The woman shook her finger at him. "You must not touch any of the arrangements. All are necessary. First, we place the cotton in the man's ears. Then, if a sorcerer calls, he will not be able to hear him. But you see, we have also sewn the lips and tied the mouth firmly shut at the top of the head. Even if the dead person should hear the sorcerer, he cannot reply. Also, you must bury him face down, too, to make speaking even more difficult. And, you see," she gestured toward the feet, "he can not walk either."

The old man eyed the director sternly. "And you must sprinkle many, many sesame seeds in the coffin as well. This will keep the dead man busy, picking them up. He will not pay attention if he is called. Above all, do not go directly to the cemetery. Weave around the town. So the dead man will be confused and cannot find his way home again. The sorcerer may look for him there."

"*Sí,*" the funeral director said resignedly, nodding his head. "I will tell the man's family that all has been done as they asked." He walked to his desk, opened a drawer, and handed some dollar bills, first to the woman, then the man. "*Gracias*, Momée, and you, Junior. I will come for you the next time there is need for your services."

3

THE FUNERAL DIRECTOR opened the side door cautiously, peered around, and the old couple slipped out into the tropical night. The uniformed policeman standing near the door waved to them as they passed.

"Come in for a moment, Terron, would you?" The director, flicking on the room's overhead lights, beckoned to the officer.

"I'm glad that you can take these night shifts when we have a body." He waved Terron to a chair near the desk. "Everyone here knows you."

As he spoke, Coret moved the body carefully onto a tray on a metal trolley, making sure he did not disturb the old people's bindings. After one quick startled glance at the trolley, the policeman kept his eyes on the neatly-piled forms on the desk. The clinical glare of the fluorescent lights gave the corpse a grislier look than the candles had. The black cloth tied around the skull contorted the face, turning it into a demonic mask. The thick threads through the lips puckered them obscenely; the protruding tufts of cotton formed enormous ears. Undisturbed, the undertaker wheeled the trolley to one of the refrigerators and expertly slid the body inside.

"I'll pay you in cash, of course," he went on as he washed his hands meticulously. "I can see it'll be necessary until those damned bodies quit turning up on the beach."

Turning on a shaded desk lamp, Coret clicked off the overhead lights and sat down heavily. "Every family

14

is imploring me to take 'special' care of their dead. My father a funeral director all his life in Loiza—I myself have been in the business for twenty years. As if Coret's Mortuary were in the habit of mislaying its customers!"

The policeman, a solid black man in his fifties with only a touch of gray in his hair and mustache, leaned back in his chair. His left eyelid had a slight droop, and as he tilted his head back, the half-closed eye glittered. "More than that, isn't it? The families are terrified someone will steal the hair or nail clippings from the body. If the wrong person has that, he's got power over the dead."

"So much of this superstition still!" the director replied. "My father always took the mourners' worries seriously, though. He was born in Haiti, you know. Came here when he was a young man. Always reassured the families that he hired only the most reliable people to lay out the bodies. Told them he himself watched the entire process. That's the way he got their business. But you know, I always suspected he half-shared their crazy notions."

The policeman said nothing but looked around at the room's modern office furnishings and the gleaming appliances.

"Well, of course, I still keep that half-corner plot empty, with a black cross on it," the director went on, a little defensively. "For Baron Samedi, the Master of Cemeteries. The plot would only be useful for a very small child, anyway. And it's only good business to leave his symbols on my mortuary sign—the gravedigger's three tools. It's small, down in the corner. People from around here know what that means—anyone else would think it natural. So many people around here still can't read."

Sighing, he moved to one of the cabinets. "Let's have a little something to warm up. Always chilly in here—necessary, you know—but this room has no windows, so the lights won't show. I don't want to give the members of this man's family the idea that people are moving around here at night. On the other hand, I keep lights on all night upstairs."

He took out a bottle of expensive Scotch, moving his hand slightly so Terron could see the label. Since even the best rum in Puerto Rico was reasonably priced, the imported Scotch had become a status symbol.

"*Salud.*" The director tilted his glass in Terron's direction. "Any progress on tracing where those five bodies come from?"

"None," the policeman said shortly. "All of the corpses were embalmed. Somebody'd be bound to miss those, you'd think. All dead of natural causes originally, the pathologists say, but all shot in the temple some time after death."

"Can't you patrol the beaches every night?"

"Man," Terron replied in disgust and scowled down into his glass. "Think about it. Four of them were dropped along that stretch of ocean between the Loiza River and Rio Grande. Gotta be four miles of beach there. Most of it deserted. Other one on the other side of the Loiza in the *Piñones*! Both places, a hundred little roads through the palm plantations to the beach. With a four-wheeler, you don't even need a road. Lots of pine trees near the beach. Anyone could slip out a few feet, throw a body down, and that quick, move back. You'd have to have an officer every five feet. And the people down there in their little shacks live pretty far apart. They're old. They go to bed early. No one's heard a thing, they say. But you don't hear much but the ocean, anyway. Big waves there in the winter."

"Any ideas yet about *why?*" Coret persisted.

"No good ones," Terron grunted. "One of the sergeants raised around here says maybe some crazy is trying to remind the people of the past, trying to scare them into taking up Voodoo more seriously again."

"It would *have* to be a crazy. Or . . . you're not thinking of an *independentista*? The ones who want to separate from the United States, take up our own culture? That kind of thing?"

"Can't imagine that, can you?" Terron scratched

his head. "It was only the freed black slaves who came here to Loiza who hung onto their old African beliefs. Well, still do, of course. But Voodoo's a little different. It's Haitian—not really a Puerto Rican thing. Not Indian. Besides, all our guy does is get a dead body, shoot it in the temple, drop it on the beach. Same gun—.25 caliber. Little hole. I guess some of the old folks on the beach would think of Voodoo, but who else would? Some of them are now thinking of moving out of their shacks and into town. But they've been living there all their lives. Got no money. Scares them, all right."

"It scares me, too." Coret leaned over the desk confidentially. "I keep thinking someone in the funeral business is trying to move in here."

Terron looked at him curiously. "You're thinking he's trying to make you look . . . what? Incompetent? But the bodies don't come from here. That's one thing we know. Advantage of a small town." He set down his empty glass.

"But suppose toward the end he gets his hands on one of mine. People would believe that maybe some of the others were, too. *You* know they aren't ours. And *I* know it, too. I went with all the other area funeral directors to look over those bodies. But will people believe that once rumor starts going? And a couple of the faces were a little deteriorated. People know that. They'd say I couldn't be sure. I'd be out of business quick."

"Well . . . I guess I can see why you might worry." Terron's half-closed eye seemed to wink ironically. "You making that much money?"

The funeral director stiffened. It crossed his mind that giving Terron the expensive Scotch might not have been such a good idea.

"I get all the local business—Catholic and Protestant."

"Exactly," Terron said comfortably. "Stranger comes in here. Locals won't trust him."

Coret relaxed. He measured a little more Scotch into each glass.

"It's true. But you can't help thinking of explanations. Somebody is going to a lot of trouble. And why? He's not covering up any crime. These people weren't murdered. And how can he be making any money pulling this stunt? Say it's some kind of morbid practical joke. He's committing a crime. It is, you know—mutilating the dead."

At that the policeman became uneasy. "*Si*—but *that* kind of crime. Our branch headquarters in Carolina is making jokes at our expense. 'In Loiza, it's so boring you have to kill people twice so they'll *know* they're dead.' That kind of thing. Well, you know the kind of problems we have here. Kids stealing tires and batteries, local car clubs driving like crazies on the Rio Grande Road, a couple burglaries. But after the third body, the papers in San Juan picked up the story. Headquarters wanted all sorts of detailed investigations. They're saying, 'Do this, do that.' And we've only got a small force here."

"But," Coret asked, "if the bodies don't come from here . . . ?"

"Just what *we* said. No evidence at all that they're *ours*. And we sent all the bodies for autopsy to the Institute of Forensic Medicine in San Juan. Nobody's claimed them. Finally they all got buried in Caguas. One thing—lucky for us, if no one else—just about then the Strangler started killing women in San Juan. Papers forgot about our bodies. When the last two showed up in January, there were only small paragraphs in the Police Blotter section of the paper."

"But now the Strangler case has been solved," the funeral director shook his head. "You think the reporters will take up our problem again?"

"Afraid so. A reporter asked the Secretary of Justice about it in his last conference. Read it in the papers. Secretary said it'd be just the job for the New York Lieutenant who caught the Strangler. Hope he was joking."

"But maybe that's an idea," Coret returned meditatively. "Balthazar Marten. Even out here, people would know his name."

"You need to know this town, this area, to find an explanation," Terron said scornfully, eying the empty glass. "Got to listen to what the people in the square are saying. Beach is empty at night unless somebody is out there up to no good. Some kid ditching a stolen car he took for a joyride. So he won't tell us, but he might have seen something and he'll tell somebody. Eventually, the word'll get back to us. But they won't tell some strange *Norteamericano*." He sniffed.

"But wait, Terron. The bodies *don't* come from here. So where do they come from? San Juan. Logical. It's only seventeen miles away. They've so many dead bodies in San Juan, they probably can't keep track of them. As you said, they ship the unclaimed ones up to Caguas—pauper's graveyard."

The funeral director was growing more pleased with his theory every minute. "Listen to me. So you get this New York guy to work on it. The Loiza office can get on with their own police work. People here will quit worrying because they'll get the idea it's nothing to do with us. Bodies just happened to get dumped on our beaches. And if any reporters show up, you can tell them it's out of your hands."

Coret paused, and looked at Terron significantly: "And if you bring in San Juan and the case never does get solved, whose fault will it be then?"

The policeman rubbed his chin. "Something in that. I'll see. Talk to the Chief."

"By the way," Coret said, getting up, "I'd appreciate it if you'd stand by the front when it gets light. People will be going to work. They'll know I'm doing what I can to take care."

4

Puerto Rico is surrounded by two large bodies of water—the Atlantic Ocean to the north, the Caribbean Sea to the south. Therefore, while all its beaches have sugar-soft sand, there are two distinct choices for the swimmer. Some beaches have waves that lap the shore as gently as the water in a bathtub when the bather moves. Other beaches appeal to the more adventurous. Particularly in winter, the Atlantic throws up waves that delight the body surfer and present a constant challenge to the swimmer. Outgoing waves collide with incoming ones. The foaming waterfall that results booms along the coast, sending the unwary sprawling end-over-end onto the shore, but lifting the alert in an exhilarating swoop.

Balthazar Marten, lieutenant of the New York Police—recently, very recently, assigned to the San Juan branch of the Puerto Rican *Policía*—looked down from the nineteenth floor of his hotel at the restless Atlantic and tried to decide whether to go for an early morning swim. He had been in Puerto Rico for two weeks and whenever he had the chance, he wanted to swim as soon as he awoke. To be more exact, he reflected, he wanted the results of an early swim.

There were all kinds of good results. His knee had been seriously injured a year before in New York by the flying metal from a car bomb that had been meant for him, but had killed his young wife, Rose, instead. The knee and certain less tangible parts of him were

20

slow to heal, but the knee, at least, quickly lost its irritating, insistent ache when he stretched it in the water. The buoyant waves required all his attention and there he could not dwell on things done and things not done. And after five minutes, the water was the perfect temperature—cool enough for a brisk swim and warm enough to be quite comfortable. He would emerge feeling healthy, virtuous, peaceful, and hungry.

But there were those first five minutes. The temperature at dawn was rarely below seventy degrees, but stepping out on the beach, he would feel a chill in the breeze. And while the first few little waves that curled around his feet would feel tepid, those that then hit his upper body were as frigid as February. No matter how often he tried it, he would always feel that the water would never warm up.

He glanced at the opaque sky. In the evening, the sun flamboyantly entered the ocean, splashing color everywhere. But in the morning, it usually returned hesitantly, offering a bit of pink here, a sliver of tangerine there, while the clouds slowly dissipated, finally unveiling the peerless blue.

The water only looks cold because it's gray, he told himself firmly. *In five minutes, it will feel wonderful*. He stepped quickly into his trunks, grabbed his robe, and hurried out of his room before he could change his mind.

Twenty minutes later, he left the ocean reluctantly. The warm waves splashed on his back, and the sand dribbled backward under his feet as if trying to pull him in again. He hardly limped at all as he made his way to the spacious, glass-enclosed terrace café that overlooked the ocean.

Technically, breakfast was not served there until 7:00 A.M. Tourists are not early risers. But the cooks came quite early to prepare the enormous daily buffet, and after the publicity of the Strangler case, they all recognized Balthazar. Like most Puerto Ricans, they found it incomprehensible that people wanted to swim in the ocean in February, even in the blazing eighty-degree afternoon. And to do it at dawn! It was not safe to swim in the ocean in months with an *r* in their names, they had pointed out to him. And, while the pool was not supposed to be open until 9:00 A.M., management would surely make an exception for the Lieutenant. It was a nice pool. . . . Was he quite sure?

But like all Puerto Ricans, they *were* sure that anyone was happier with lots of food. So the waiter unlocked the door of the empty café with a broad smile and beckoned Balthazar in. In a few minutes, he was brought cold, sweet pineapple juice and hot, creamy coffee. The waiter placed a platter heaped with a variety of breakfast rolls before him, soon followed by a large plate of moist, fluffy scrambled eggs. Uncovering a silver tray, he invited Balthazar to choose from plump, brown sausages, crisp bacon, pink slices of ham. Unable to decide, Balthazar sampled all three.

It was still too early for the morning newspapers but, Balthazar thought, generously buttering a croissant, that was just as well. He needed no distractions from his thoughts. The morning spread smoothly before him.

He felt ready for his assigned case. Two weeks earlier he had left New York glumly, unenthusiastic about being sent, however briefly, to San Juan, uninterested in checking out Mafia infiltration in a gambling casino in the city. At the time he had even tried to refuse, half-suspecting that Captain Mike Helmsley might have arranged the temporary transfer to see if Balthazar's knee might heal, away from the frozen streets of New York. And, to see, Balthazar now admitted to himself, if he might return to the living.

For, given the change in himself over the last two weeks, he realized that for the past year, he had been numb, almost anesthetized. He had not been able to recover from Rose's death, had not been able to summon up his previous intense interest in his work. He had turned bleakly away from any plans for the future, concentrating instead on getting through each unappetizing day. Had someone told him a few weeks could make a difference in his attitude, he would have responded that such a philosophy belonged only to television's situation comedies.

Last night, MacAtee had even commented on the change in him. T., his oldest friend, a practical and extremely successful New York bookie, resting up in San Juan after the strenuous action of the Super Bowl, had come close to an uncharacteristic serious personal remark. "Balls, you look like a new guy. I told you you'd like PR. Something to do with walking around in February with a whole bunch of fine ladies half-dressed, not bundled up to the nose like back home. Some only a *tenth* dressed. God is good. As the nuns used to tell us."

Coming in from cold weather and warming up, one first feels a tingling in the fingertips and, Balthazar reflected, that described his present mental sensation. Since he'd arrived, he had done some useful work in San Juan. And he had met Maira Knight. One, of course, did not fall in love that quickly. After all, he had known her for barely two weeks. And besides, she was technically married. Her husband's plane had been shot down ten years before in Vietnam but he was still listed as MIA. But now . . .

He sipped his second cup of coffee slowly. Perhaps even a refusal to borrow pain from the future was a good sign, too. It meant that there was hope that problems might eventually be solved, that things might work out. It meant that one wanted an unclouded today because today had pleasant prospects. He signed for his breakfast and walked out the door, unaware that his face wore an expansive smile.

The plump, middle-aged cashier at the upstairs registration desk smiled too, as she saw the tall American slowly cross the lobby and head towards the elevator. Look how much better that man looks now, she thought. So different from when he came—sallow, lines around the eyes, no meat on his bones. In that robe he looked a little fatter, but still too thin. If he filled out more, she considered, he would be very handsome.

At first she had wondered if he might be Hispanic—dark hair, a touch of olive in his skin. His first name, too, *Baltasar*, a very common name in Puerto Rico, although he didn't spell it that way. And he spoke excellent Spanish. But when she asked, he said, "No, Irish and Dutch." Very polite, he was.

She sighed, and slipping off a high-heeled shoe, rubbed an aching foot against her ankle. She needed another husband herself, and she was definitely not interested in thin, intense young men in their middle thirties. She wanted a man like José, her first husband. Only this one should have a pension. A businessman, she decided, near retirement. Like that nice Señor Johnson in 1016. It was the third time he'd been down, and he seemed lonely. Always wanted to stop and talk. And he said he was a widower. She smoothed her dress over her ample hips and ampler bosom and hummed a little salsa tune.

5

SIXTO CARDENAS, a detective on the Homicide One Squad of the Puerto Rican *Policía*, pulled his unmarked Chevrolet Nova into the circular drive in front of the Dupont Hotel, drove past the hotel's Registration unloading zone, and turned off the motor. Spreading his fingers, he lifted the dark hair from his forehead. His thin young face wore the faint frown of anxiety which always marks the foreheads of the overly conscientious. He stared unseeingly at the carefully landscaped perimeter, blooming with pale orange, bright pink, and dark purple bougainvillea. He was thinking regretfully that it was probably the last time he would be picking up the Lieutenant in the morning.

Simple luck had dictated their working together in the last two weeks. "Such good luck for me," Sixto had told his mother that morning at breakfast.

"Lucky for that Lieutenant from New York," his mother had returned indignantly. "Without you——"

"Mama, I know what you will say, but you must see how it is. I have only been out of the Police Academy five years. Chief Villareal assigns me to this case, to that case. I interview people, check on details. I write my report. But Lieutenant Marten . . . ," despite Balthazar's urgings, Sixto found it hard to think of him as *Baltasar*, "he is a *famous* detective. You saw the newspapers in the Strangler case, how they all said the Lieutenant was 'an expert in such cases.' And he asks for my ideas. He is very intelligent. I learned——"

25

"But then you must tell Chief Villareal," his mother had cut in firmly, "that you wish to continue working with Lieutenant Marten, Sixto. The Lieutenant will want that, too. After what you have done—"

"*Mira*, Mama," Sixto tried once more. "The Lieutenant was sent here from New York to work on a case for the American *Policía*. His work does not involve the Puerto Ricans." He stopped, trying to think of a way to explain to his mother how the Lieutenant had come to be assigned briefly to the Puerto Rican Homicide One Squad.

"You understand, it was the Secretary of Justice, not Chief Villareal, not even Captain Almon, who—"

"Then you must speak to *El Señor* Secretary, Sixto. He will know who you are now, your picture in all the newspapers. Your handsome face on the television. The neighbors say . . . I can tell you that even Senora Ramirez whose son makes so many thousands at Eli Lilly stopped me in the market, and if she ever even nodded at me before I don't remember, and she say, 'Your son has done good work.' " Señora Cardenas pursed her lips in remembered satisfaction.

Sixto kissed her on one plump cheek and hurried out the door.

But even if, he mused, the Lieutenant needed a driver still, Villareal would surely appoint a new recruit, not send a detective. The Lieutenant was now familiar with San Juan, and although it was not so easy because of his knee, it was possible for him to drive himself. . . .

Balthazar climbed into Sixto's car, greeting him with mock severity. "And how many times must I tell you to inform the bellman when you arrive so that they can call me? The taxpayers of San Juan need their most valuable man on the streets preventing crime, not daydreaming in hotel driveways."

"We have a new program, Lieutenant," Sixto grinned. "We have the taxpayers of New York send here a detective who will end all crime."

"Good idea! When is he coming?"

Sixto pulled into the dense traffic of the Condado, the tourist section of San Juan. They moved by inches up *Avenida* Ashford. The narrow Condado with its sweeping view of the Atlantic had once been an exclusive residential district. There were still a few large, exquisitely-cared-for houses on shaded streets. But when Castro's Cuba said "Yanqui, No!" the tourists simply flew a little farther—to Puerto Rico's equally sunny shores. Luxury hotels now blossomed on the Condado. Cars clogged the streets.

Balthazar stared out the window, peacefully thinking that even rush hour traffic is easier to take in the sunshine. In New York you had to be sternly committed to survival before you walked out the door. Here, you could wait, see how things turned out, let the pleasures of life persuade you. Paradise.

The only regret he had was that on his new assignment at the casino he would have no partner. It was a real regret. He wanted to tell Sixto how much he valued the young detective's friendship and abilities—most of all, the fact that Sixto knew how to move quickly—and when not to move at all.

He was still thinking about what to say when they pulled up to the imposing, marble-based skyscraper that housed the San Juan *Policía*. He cleared his throat. "Just like the last case," he said, avoiding Sixto's eyes, "I started with an interview with Captain Almon. It certainly didn't turn out the way I expected then." He paused, stared out the windshield. "I'll miss working with you." Balthazar got out of the car hurriedly.

Two weeks ago, at their first meeting, Almon had been formal, gravely polite. But then he had been more embarrassed than anything else, explaining to Balthazar how it happened that a New York police lieutenant sent on an undercover gambling investigation case had been instead assigned on arrival to a Puerto Rican homicide case. He had been apologetic and tactful. Balthazar had been impressed with Almon's restraint in what must have been a very difficult situation.

Today he rose, shook Balthazar's hand, and waved him to a chair, not looking at him directly. Odd, Balthazar thought as he sat down, he seems as awkward now as he did when we first met. His mouth pursed, he stared at the contents of a manila folder on his desk.

The captain was a trim man in his early forties. His bearing, even when seated, was erect, and his uniform always looked as if it had been made to measure. He turned the file pages slowly, but his jaws were tense. It occurred to Balthazar that Almon was very, very angry. At last he looked up.

"I don't know how to tell you this except straight-forwardly, Lieutenant Marten. There is a peculiar and vaguely troublesome case in a small town near San Juan. Because it is so unusual, it has unfortunately attracted the attention of the media. You may even recall, although I would doubt it, that a reporter jokingly remarked at the last press conference you held with Secretary of Justice Cortes that you would be the ideal man for the Loiza case." He paused, his jaw tightening.

"I'm afraid, Captain, that I don't. . . ."

"No, you could not have assumed it had anything to do with you or your presence here. For it does not. But the Secretary of Justice was intrigued by the suggestion. And you will certainly recall how much he wishes to cooperate with the members of the press. In brief, he has, without consulting us, assured the press that you will look into the case."

The captain went on hurriedly, looking down again at the folder. "One of course wishes to maintain good relations with the Justice Department. And it is always a little difficult when a new secretary takes office. Although that department has nothing, I repeat nothing, to do with your investigations—unless there is some question of police malpractice, of course—certain lines have always to be redrawn."

He pushed his chair back abruptly, his eyes fixed on his stubby hands, which were clenched on his desk.

"In the first instance, your involvement was at least understandable, so I said nothing. This time . . . I had a long conference with our Superintendent of Police. He quite agrees with my position. But it seems that the Secretary had already called your New York office and obtained your Captain Helmsley's permission. No doubt Captain Helmsley was put in a most difficult position." He continued to study his hands.

"You mean, Captain, that the Secretary wishes me to work on another homicide case before going on to the gambling invest—"

"It is not a homicide case." Almon's voice was icy.

He stood and walked to a wall which held a large map of the Caribbean. In outline the shape of Puerto Rico always looked to Balthazar like an unfinished sculpture. The artist had started with a thick rectangle of clay and had fashioned a clever baboon's head on the northwest corner, then moved south and added paws; but he just barely started rounding off the eastern half before wandering off, planning no doubt to complete it another day. The baboon faced the rear end of the crab-shaped island of Hispaniola, which contained the Dominican Republic and Haiti. The pincers of Haiti nipped at Cuba's shore.

Almon jabbed his finger at the top of the northeastern part of Puerto Rico, where the million and a half people of metropolitan San Juan cluster around the rich port that gives the island its name. "Let me explain this first. Old San Juan is one of the most ancient cities in the Western Hemisphere, but much of the surrounding area remained small farms until quite recently. Look at Bayamón, for example."

His finger moved to that city just slightly south of San Juan. "Now Bayamón is very modern, many factories, 200,000 people. But until after the Second World War, it was rural, just dirt roads with ox-carts on them. Some places near San Juan have not changed like Bayamón has, Lieutenant, although some have. In between, there are . . . pockets. See here, have you been yet to Fajardo?"

"Yes," Balthazar said, remembering how much that town, with its high-rise apartments and thousands of small pleasure boats had reminded him of San Diego. Fajardo was very near the large U.S. Navy base at Roosevelt Roads, and he had thought the servicemen must have created that Southern California look.

"You went, no doubt, straight across from San Juan on Highway 3?"

"I did. I was told the other way, driving along the seacoast, was very beautiful, but extremely slow."

"That is right," the Captain nodded. "In fact, if you take the coastal route, you must even wait for the hand-pulled ferry to take you across the Loiza River."

"Really?" Balthazar was surprised. "A *hand-pulled* ferry? For cars? But it can't be much more than fifteen miles from San Juan and twenty from Fajardo."

"*Si*, construction has begun, but there is no bridge there yet, and Loiza is some distance off the main road. So the area is much as it was forty—or even one hundred and forty—years ago. It's very close to San Juan, but far away in other ways, you understand. There are many old people in Loiza. People live there who would have grown up with ox-carts. It is still very primitive." Still staring at the map, he added meditatively, "No doubt that explains all the dead chickens."

Balthazar was silent. Surely he was not being sent to investigate the poultry industry. Would Helmsley ever have. . . .

Almon turned back to his desk. "The problem is that, over the last few months, five bodies have been found near Loiza."

"Excuse me, Captain, you do mean dead *people*? This is a homicide case, then?"

"No. At least we have found no indication that any of the bodies were homicide victims. The cause of death in every case was natural. But at some time after death the body was shot through the temple—each time with the same small caliber gun—and placed on the beaches near Loiza."

Almon thrust the file folder at Balthazar, still avoiding his eyes. "Here is all the information that I have. Secretary Cortes will be here soon. He would like to see you. The agreement that the Superintendent and I have come to is that, in the interests of . . . ah . . . interdepartmental harmony, you could take a few days and visit the area. We have explained firmly to the Secretary that we can only spare you for a week, Lieutenant. The Secretary has promised us, in turn, that this pre-emption of your time will not be repeated."

Almon stood up. His relief that the conference was ending was evident. "Given that time frame, we would not expect any real progress. We have so many crimes against the living that this may seem less urgent. Still, I understand the local people there are terrified. It is not a joke to them. But the joker may soon tire of his game, if that's what this is all about. In the meantime, we will be seen to have taken some action to reassure people."

Almon moved briskly toward his office door. "When the Secretary arrives, he wishes to talk to you in the tenth-floor conference room. In the meantime, you will have an opportunity to look over these reports."

He opened the door, and ushered Balthazar through. "Loiza is a singularly beautiful area. If you like, I can have Agente Cardenas take you there. You seem to work well together."

At last his dark eyes focused on Balthazar. "Once again I apologize, Lieutenant." After shaking hands, he shut his door quietly.

Balthazar stood in the hallway, looking at the closed door, thinking that Helmsley must be laughing his ass off in New York. Balthazar sincerely hoped it was snowing heavily there.

6

SECRETARY OF JUSTICE CORTES had an imposing head. His thick dark hair was only lightly touched with gray; his dark, expressive eyes were emphasized by his over-sized glasses. His mustache, also graying, was well trimmed—not too large or too thin—and it outlined his rather full lips. Any casting director would have taken one look and thought: *important public official*.

But he was an experienced Puerto Rican politician. Although Balthazar had known him only a short time, he realized that one should not underestimate the kind of intelligence that was required for such survival. The Secretary was in great demand as a speaker. He could strip ideas of their complexity and reclothe them in quotable language. He was very accessible to the media. On slow news days journalists called on him, and therefore he was extremely popular with reporters. Therefore, perhaps, he was also very popular with the people.

He stood and shook Balthazar's hand warmly. "A true pleasure to work with you again, Lieutenant, even if we have been given such a constricted time frame. Our press has become fascinated by this case. Needless to say, the Puerto Rican public is horrified by it. And of course it is quite disturbing for the people in the area, too. We would all be grateful for any insights you might have."

"I would be happy to do what I can," Balthazar replied. In New York he had rarely been involved with the administration and public relations of police work.

But he had learned quickly. One said something quite positive and then hurried to qualify it. "I must say it seems to call for someone with an intimate knowledge of the area and the people."

"Oh, exactly," Cortes beamed. "And the Loiza people are prepared to fill you in—delighted to have your help. I just finished talking with Sergeant Terron there. Good man—been on the case from the beginning. He quite agrees with you, but he noted that perhaps an outsider with a fresh eye could see what other investigators have missed.

"Now," He picked up a yellow legal pad on which several words and phrases were neatly printed in block capitals. "You've had an opportunity to look over the file? Good. Let me give you some additional background."

Balthazar, an accomplished upside-down reader, saw the words printed on the pad. VOODOO. SLAVERY: 1) HORROR OF, 2) HISTORY. He groaned inwardly. His eyes glazed. He closed them briefly and mentally revised the picture he had had of Helmsley and the snowstorm in Manhattan. It was now icy, stinging sleet.

"Voodoo," the Secretary intoned. He looked at Balthazar solemnly, and without losing eye contact, took off his glasses.

For the next twenty minutes, Balthazar received a thorough indoctrination on this subject. He learned about the nature spirits called *loa*, about Baron Samedi, and about the need to kill the dead all over again lest they become *zombis*. He endured a detailed description of Voodoo ceremonies. He was told that all Voodoo believers were also good Roman Catholics who saw no conflict between that religion and the traditional ideas of their African ancestors.

The Secretary paused, tapped the word *SLAVERY* and shook his head sorrowfully. "The blacks brought here to work in the Americas in the cane fields, on the coffee and banana plantations, were brutally treated. They were terrified—and confused. Torn from the green freedom of their jungle homes, they could not understand what had happened to them."

Along with the sleet pelting the sidewalks, Balthazar envisioned gale-force winds howling through the skyscraper canyons.

"So," the Secretary gestured, "the slaves clung to their old explanations about bad luck. While both the Spanish and French governments required them to be baptized on arrival, they were given no instruction in the Catholic faith. The plantation owners hardly felt it was wise to encourage the idea of the brotherhood of man.

"Here were these poor slaves," he continued earnestly, "and there was that faraway white man's God, and the scarcely less distant saints and angels. So the blacks turned to their old gods, whom they thought of as . . . middle-level managers who could protect them."

Balthazar solemnly digested the information that Puerto Rico had never had many slaves, unlike Haiti, for example, and that when the Puerto Rican slaves were freed in 1873, most of them went to the area that is now Loiza Aldea. And that now many of these slaves' descendants believed, absolutely, in some form of Voodoo. "I use that term loosely, Lieutenant. It's actually a Haitian word. Of course Haitians who came to Puerto Rico often went to Loiza," the Secretary added.

Eight below zero, Balthazar thought, plus the wind chill factor.

At last the Secretary rose. "You will find Sergeant Terron also helpful on these matters. Now, as long as you have only a week, I've made a few arrangements to save you time. You and Cardenas should surely stay out there for the entire week. It's a very time-consuming drive, even though it's not far mile-wise. There's a government-sponsored resort right in Loiza. On the beach. Nice spot, Terron tells me, two bedrooms with bath and kitchenette. Restaurant's not open when they're not busy. And, of course, they're practically empty now since it's winter. But it has a swimming pool."

His voice deepened; sincerity required a richer tone. "All of us appreciate your assistance, Lieutenant, and I believe this case calls for a man of your particular abilities. I see it very much as an armchair puzzle. There will be no danger to you or the people there, I'm sure. Brains are needed, the application of intelligence."

He shook Balthazar's hand gravely.

7

BALTHAZAR HAD THE MAP of Puerto Rico spread out on his knees. He and Sixto were driving to Loiza through Isla Verde, a section of Carolina Township that merges into San Juan's urban sprawl. Isla Verde is neither an island nor green. Nor were Balthazar and Sixto actually driving. They were sitting in the brown Chevrolet Nova which was sitting in the middle of a street choked with heavy road-building equipment, a crowd of pedestrians, and a great many other equally stationary cars. Whenever the traffic crept forward slightly, a car pulled out of one of the many driveways of the high condominium buildings or hotels that lined the beach—and blocked all view of it—on the left. There was very little progress.

The road crew moved their ponderous machines up and down the middle of the street. Waved on by a few shirtless flagmen in bright yellow hard hats, cars and buses inched their way down the narrow corridor on each side between the roadwork and the parked cars. Most of the pedestrians were dressed only in swim suits and lights shirts; they were burdened with beach paraphernalia—folding chairs, beach balls, soft drink coolers, large picnic hampers. Many were very attractive girls. The drivers waved them cheerfully across the street in front of them.

The patrons of the many small outdoor bars that lined the street across from the high-rises wandered over to the stranded cars with plastic glasses in their hands. They chatted with their traffic-bound friends, often sharing their drinks. The sun was overhead in an unclouded sky. Most of the people were smiling.

"This looks more like an ongoing block party than a main street," Balthazar remarked. Sixto had his fingers spread, and he was happily thunking the inside of his knuckles and the heels of his hands against the steering wheel to a fast *merengue* beat blasting from a suitcase-sized stereo perched on a nearby bar stool. Although he had expressed the slight disdain and deep suspicion of a born city-dweller for country life, his pleasure at their mutual assignment had been so evident that Balthazar himself was somewhat cheered. The nature of the case, however, pleased neither of them.

"Many parties in Isla Verde," Sixto replied. "Many young people here. Everybody is very relaxed. But, too, today is Monday and some of the people might have the day off. This weekend was the feast of *Nuestra Señora de la Candelaria*."

"Our Lady of the Bonfires?"

"*Sí*, you burn up old things from your house. And dance, too." The young Puerto Rican was humming.

"A spring-cleaning party?"

"*Sí*, but one goes to church, maybe. . . . Some do. . . . Well, my mother does." He shrugged. "They say that Puerto Rico is the only Catholic country without a religion."

Two teenaged girls cut agilely in front of their car. They were wearing tropical print swimsuits cut up on their thighs almost to their waists and down the middle to their navels. There were breathtaking bulges everywhere. The girls waved and giggled. The men watched them in silence. The roadworkers brought their machines to abrupt stops and stared—not in silence. Everyone waited until the girls had disappeared from view.

"Um," said Balthazar, "I thought no one swam in February?"

"They are not going to *swim*," Sixto replied courteously. "They're going to the *beach*."

"Oh," said Balthazar. "Which beach?"

"The people walking here are going to the one that faces the condos and hotels. There are no private beaches in Puerto Rico. Anyone can use them."

"That's right. But isn't that beach awfully crowded?"

"Oh, *sí*. That's why everyone goes there. But many of these people in the cars are going to the big *Balneario Publico Isla Verde* up ahead. The public beaches have showers and toilets. Families like that. Once we get by that, we'll move much faster."

"The trouble is, Sixto, that I don't see where we're moving *to*. There is no road shown on this map after we pass the public beach and go into this big green section marked *Piñones*."

"I have not been this way, myself. But Diaz was stationed at the Carolina branch for some time and he says it's the best way for us to go this afternoon, or we'll get caught in the rush on Highway 3. He says it's a beautiful drive, and taking the ferry across the river is a good introduction to Loiza Aldea. He laughed when he said it, but he insisted there was a road. Then Captain Almon said, too, that we should go this way because we can take a look at one of the beaches where a body was discovered."

At last they swung onto the wide *Avenida Boca de Cangrejos*—literally Mouth of the Crab Avenue—a four-lane highway with a large median. The San Juan Airport—officially re-named Luis Muñoz Marin Airport—was hidden behind the bushes on their right. On their left was an enormous paved parking lot for the beach. Balthazar was about to comment on the number of driver-instruction cars weaving erratically around the almost empty lot, when a huge 747 roared in for a landing. It looked terrifyingly near; Balthazar felt he could reach out and touch the wing tip. Then he looked the other way.

"Good Lord. Look. There must be at least a hundred people selling food on the other side of the highway."

Some of the vendors had elaborate stands with portable generators that turned whole chickens on spits; others had the generators hooked to blenders to mix *pina coladas*. Still others had large charcoal braziers on which to cook *pinchos*—barbecued pork or beef on small wooden skewers. There were shiny metal New York style hot dog machines and big pots of sizzling fat sitting on burners, ready to make *alcapurrias*—mashed plantains and pork or crab wrapped in batter. There was also a battered Volkswagen bus with a beaded curtain and a sign: Tarot Card Reader.

"*Sí*," Sixto said, glancing at the stands. "For the people at the beach."

"Well, if this continues, we don't have to worry about going hungry."

"There will be food stands, I am sure," Sixto grinned, "but we would never have to worry about going hungry. My mother believes they do not have food in the country. She has packed food for the week. From what I saw when I put the box in the trunk, I think truly for many weeks."

"Did she make any more of those pralines?" Balthazar asked with interest.

"Pralines?"

"Those round things with the sugar on the bottom and the coconut curls on the top?"

"*Dulce de coco*. Of course," Sixto said. "We also have sheets, towels—"

"Sheets and towels? Aren't we going to be staying in some sort of a resort?"

"My mama inquired of the neighbors after I called her. They say that these things are not provided. The government-sponsored resorts are very inexpensive so that families can afford vacations. Families must bring all necessary items."

"These are little cabins or something?"

Sixto shook his head slowly.

As they left Isla Verde, the broad highway led onto a two-lane bridge that crossed over a small bay. There was an attractive yacht club on the edge of the water and a rustic seafood restaurant. The inlet was filled with boats, mainly small, fast, private deep-sea fishing boats.

But after they left the bridge, the highway ended

abruptly. At first it split obligingly into two one-way lanes that veered around a large decrepit building sitting directly in the middle of the road. The old outdoor cafe was wooden with rusty beer signs hanging on its exterior. When the road merged again, it was asphalt, narrow and partly covered with sand.

Balthazar looked around in amazement. They were only forty yards from the yacht club, and over his left shoulder he could see the tall shining buildings of Isla Verde lining the ocean. But the contrast between that modern suburb and this rural section was immediate and extreme.

As they drove on, they could see a few scattered well-built concrete houses, but these stood next to lean-tos with people lounging in their doorways. Some shacks stood so close to the road that their interiors, stacked with old furniture, were visible. Yards surrounded by makeshift cactus fences held chickens and a grunting pig or two. Sixto had to slow constantly to avoid potholes and the cattle and small delicate goats that wandered untended across the road.

Swiftly, the houses disappeared. On their left stretched wide palm fields, and behind the rows of palms rose an impenetrable wall of mangroves, their roots climbing in all directions. On their right was a high sand embankment, scattered with tall palms. They seemed to be driving through a green tunnel, but when the embankment dipped, they could see miles of deserted, but perfect, sandy beaches.

"I don't think we're in Kansas any more," Balthazar said wryly. "But it doesn't look like Puerto Rico, either. More like a jungle. And it makes what I was telling you about the Secretary's ideas on Voodoo a little more believable."

"Maybe," Sixto answered dubiously. "I did not think Puerto Ricans practiced Voodoo. Now, Haitians. And . . . maybe Jamaicans . . . and . . . mmm . . . people in Brazil. But we Puerto Ricans are the descendants of the Taino Indians. I studied this in a history class when I was very young. Several times I had this in a history class." He sighed.

"The Taino Indians? I thought the Caribbean was named for some other Indians."

"The Carib Indians. They were warriors. Not the Tainos. They were "the Good People." That's what Taino means. They stayed here and grew things like . . . like . . . peanuts. And peppers."

"What did they believe?"

"They had ceremonies in ballparks. Played a game like soccer."

"Ballparks?"

"*Sí,*" Sixto insisted. "There is one still somewhere on the island." He waved his hand vaguely and then put it quickly back on the wheel as the car hit an enormous pothole. "And they prayed to trees. And rocks."

They rounded a corner and suddenly the road widened slightly and they were in the midst of a small community. A modern elementary school, its yard filled with bright yellow school buses, crowded the road. A sign outside a square concrete building next to it indicated that this was the headquarters of the Mounted Police.

The road grew momentarily better and then much worse as they bumped through the palm fields again. Balthazar pointed to one of the little goats grazing by the side of the road. "In important Voodoo ceremonies, they sacrifice one of these goats, instead of just chickens. Slit their throats, even drink their blood."

Sixto looked at Balthazar.

"Then," Balthazar went on, sharing his new expertise, "they cook them and eat them."

"Oh," Sixto's face cleared. "I had some barbecued goat. A young one. Very good."

"Goat? Well, I suppose. My Dutch aunt thought Americans were crazy because they wouldn't eat horse meat. She said that in stores in Belgium and Holland it was sold just like pork or beef, and that, especially in cabbage soup, it was better than beef."

"Ugh," Sixto said. "*Horse* meat?"

The ocean disappeared again behind the embankment until that dipped, revealing a wide, sand-encircled cove. In the middle rocked an almost toy-like red-and-white tugboat. A solitary fisherman stood on the shore. He whirled a heavy weight around and around above his head and, darting forward like a javelin thrower, hurled it a hundred yards into the water. He held tightly to the fat reel of fishing line in his other hand. "This where the body was found, you think?" Sixto asked.

"Well, they described the location in the report as rock-lined and small. This beach is pretty big."

A short distance on, they saw a smaller one, fenced in by high rock cliffs. The only sign of life was a black frigate bird wheeling high overhead. They had not seen even another car for some time.

"That's probably it," Balthazar remarked. "You can see the problem. Somebody could be here half the night, stacking bodies like cordwood. Who'd see him?"

"Nobody drives this road at night," Sixto said flatly. "Not during the day either, it seems. Which is a good thing because there is no place to pull over to let another car past."

"I thought this whole stretch was only eleven miles long."

Sixto checked his watch. "We have been driving for twenty min—"

A huge, dirty-gray Brahma bull, its eyes rolling wildly, came charging around the next curve, down the middle of the road, heading straight for their car. Sixto honked, braked, and veered to the right. The car came to a sudden stop on the soft shoulder of the road. The bull went racing by without stopping.

Sixto pressed down the accelerator, gently, hopefully. The sound was unmistakeable. One tire spun uselessly in the sand. The car didn't budge. Sixto tried again, gritting his teeth. The motor raced. The Chevrolet was stuck.

Balthazar got out and leaned over to look. The

right rear tire was half a hubcap deep in loose sand. Sixto walked around and gazed down in disgust.

"Diaz may call this a road," he said, "but the mapmakers of Puerto Rico do not, and I also do not."

They eyed the tire. The last house had been a few miles back, and that had been a deserted-looking shack. The only sound was the woosh of the surf, the background clatter of insects, and the rustle of the breeze through the high bushes with huge fan-like leaves which edged the road. "If we jacked this up a bit and stuck some dry branches under it, we'd get some traction," Balthazar suggested.

Sixto opened the trunk and handed the tools to Balthazar. "I will go back to the palm field," he said glumly, and trudged around the curve.

Balthazar bent over, gingerly putting his weight on his knee. He scooped the sand from around the tire and put down the tools.

Then he looked just behind the tire, and saw four pairs of dirty tennis shoes.

He glanced up. Four young men looked down at him, smiling. Two were blacks with some Puerto Rican blood, and two were Puerto Ricans with dark skin and kinky hair.

One of the two blacks, a burly teen-ager wearing a sweatshirt cut off at the armpits to display heavily-muscled arms, shifted his gum from one side of his mouth to the other. "*Pinché, mano?*"

"Felipe, Felipe," one of the Puerto Ricans, who seemed slightly older, stepped forward and hit his friend lightly on the arm. "You are a stupid. The *caballero* is a *turista*. He does not speak Spanish. I, José Jimenez, will translate. My friend here," he said, with a wide smile, "he say to you, 'You got trouble, brother?' "

Balthazar stood up, careful to keep his weight off his injured knee, and brushed the sand off his hands. His eyes flicked over the bulge, covered with a large red rag, in the back of Felipe's pocket.

The other young Puerto Rican let out a high-pitched giggle. His ears lay flat against his head at the top, but flared forward in the middle, as if he had been repeatedly lifted by his earlobes as a child. His cheeks were covered with fresh pimples, dry scabs of pimples, and scars from others which had healed. He pointed to the Chevrolet's model name, in script on the back of the trunk. "Nova." The others snickered.

José turned with a grin and said to Balthazar, "*No va.* In Spanish that means it does not go. Your Chevvie *does* not go."

"Perhaps," Balthazar began, "you would. . . ."

José raised his hand. "Say no more. We are the *turista* welcoming committee. For the whole *Piñones* area. Very, very often, others have this same problem. These bulls, you know, are very easily frightened. The fences are not much. People are careless. But we are here to help."

Felipe leaned over and hefted the tire iron. He handed it to José. Then he took a step closer to Balthazar. He was not as tall as the detective, but he was much broader.

"Now," José went on, lightly tapping the tire iron against his palm, never taking his unsmiling eyes from Balthazar, "Felipe here is very strong. Strong as a bull, you see. You would be surprised how grateful all the *turistas* are for our help. They are very, very generous. Sometimes they just give us all the money in their billfolds. Imagine that—just for a little help. Sometimes they give us the whole billfold. We do not take traveler's checks, though."

He turned to his friends, put his hand on his hip, held his wrist limply, and pantomimed carrying a purse. They laughed. "Sometimes," he continued, "the ladies even give us their handbags. But we say, 'No, no, we don't need these.' No one complains, you see, because we are very polite. And it would be very troublesome—and expensive—to get a tow truck."

José hit his palm again with the tire iron. "But it is not necessary for your friend to get the branches. We had better tell him, hadn't we? You go, Jaime." He gestured toward the pimply-faced youth. "You had better go with him, Jorge."

The two loped off in the direction Sixto had taken. "You see," José continued conversationally, "it is very dangerous out here. We always go in pairs. The police here ride horses. Just like the cavalry in the movies, no? But where are the police when you need them, I always say. They never come rescuing you like the cavalry when you have trouble like this. Car trouble, I mean, of course."

"We are . . ." Balthazar began, reaching toward his hip pocket for his police identification. Felipe's arm shot out quickly and swept Balthazar's arm aside.

"Pardon, pardon," José said with a smirk. "It's just that we get nervous when people reach for things. So dangerous, as I said. Do you know that many people now even carry guns in their back pockets? Knives, sometimes too."

Sixto rounded the bushes, the two teenagers on each side of him. His jaw muscles quivered, but his young face was expressionless. One of the teenagers with him called out in Spanish, "Today, we are helping the *gobiernos*, José."

José looked at Balthazar's face in some surprise. "An American *gobierno*?" He reached over and delicately lifted Balthazar's trouser leg and glanced at the gun strapped to the boot. His nose crinkled fastidiously. He carefully brushed Balthazar's trouser leg where he had touched it.

"How lucky for us that we can be of service, isn't that right, my friends? Especially to two such fine *gobiernos*. Who would have thought it by just looking? Usually, even if you do not have a nice blue and white car with the nice round insignia that says *Gobierno de Puerto Rico* on it, we can tell."

His dark eyes regarded Balthazar thoughtfully. "*Gobierno* means government. Sometimes we refer to the police that way. No disrespect, of course. Well, well. But *you* must not think of offering us any money under the circumstances. No, no. If you will both get in the car, we can all push. We will make sure your Nova goes. No trouble at all. We are only too happy to help."

Sixto and Balthazar climbed back into the car, Sixto started the motor, and the young men applied enthusiastic muscle to the bumper. As they drove off, all four raised their arms, waving goodbye exaggeratedly.

Sixto was still swearing softly when they saw the quick-moving, dark brown river ahead.

8

THEY PULLED UP behind a battered pickup truck, its bed almost completely filled by a huge hog, sitting on its haunches. There was a rope tied around his neck, but the enormous animal was perfectly still; only his tail swished occasionally at a fly. He seemed to be enjoying the outing. The old driver, too, looked contented. He was outside the truck, leaning against the hood, sipping on a beer, squinting across the river at the barge on the other side. It was hard to tell if he was a light-skinned black man or a sun-weathered Puerto Rican. His narrowed eyes were red-veined and the cracks in his cheeks were as deep as furrows.

"Is that the ferry, *El Ancon*?" Sixto asked, stretching gratefully as he got out of the car.

"*Sí.*" The man gestured toward the other side with his beer can.

"Have you been waiting long?"

The man shifted his gaze down river to the north where the Loíza river poured into the blue Atlantic. He seemed to be measuring distance, not time.

"*Sí*," he said. "Not busy. But, *mira*, there are already two cars waiting on the other side to cross." The old man's Spanish was difficult for Balthazar to understand because all the word endings were dropped. "Now there are two waiting there and two here, *El Ancon* may come soon. They charge $2.50 a car."

Balthazar looked upriver to the south. The half-constructed bridge gleamed white in the sunlight. On

47

each side of the river were tall, thick concrete I-beams, but no middle span yet connected them. Through the huge missing piece, one could see the green mountains. To the east rose a high gray mountain, its peak completely obscured by thick clouds.

"That's where the Rain Forest is? Is that mountain *El Yunque*?" he asked.

The old man turned to squint at him. He eyed his Puerto Rican loose shirt, then looked at his face, and again at his shirt. He seemed puzzled. "*Sí, El Yunque* is covered with clouds always."

"There's a good road up the mountain, I understand."

"So I have heard," the old man replied reluctantly, rubbing his thumb against the beer can. He paused and then asked Balthazar, "You are no a *turista*?"

"No," Balthazar replied.

"Some *turistas* come this way, but no many. To eat the crab."

A shiny blue Toyota now pulled up behind those waiting on the other side. Two young men sauntered out of the bar next to the cars. They began waving the cars slowly up the small steel tailgate of the ferry. A stooped older man, clinging to his frail wife's arm, shuffled out of the bar and boarded the ferry. The two held tightly to the railing on the downriver side. Two gray-haired men who had been squatting on each side of the raft-like ferry pulled up some wire traps and emptied them into big white paint buckets. The barge was pushed off and moved almost imperceptibly across the hundred yards of river that separated the shores. As it approached, Balthazar watched the young men hauling at the rope with precise movements and unhurried grace. Ten minutes later, the ramp thunked down. The cars drove off carefully, and the old couple inched toward a crumbling stone bench next to a decrepit shack.

After the ferry was reloaded, Balthazar walked forward to talk again to the old farmer, who was gazing with satisfaction at his hog. When the detective complimented him on the size of the animal, the man cackled with pleasure. He explained that his old one had recently died, but that he was able to trade for a new hog because so many people wanted his young pigs to roast for the feast day. They both contemplated the animal, who was now looking philosophically at the water. Casually, Balthazar inquired about the discovery of the bodies on the beach.

The old man's gap-toothed smile disappeared. Balthazar could almost smell his fear. Without meeting Balthazar's eyes, he asked, "You *gobierno*?"

"Yes," Balthazar answered.

The old farmer mumbled a few phrases, and then stared out at the water, refusing to answer any further questions.

Balthazar joined Sixto, who stood watching the two bargemen as they tugged rhythmically at the fat rope that was tied to the opposite shore. One of the young men, a handsome black with wide shoulders and a small gold earring in his right earlobe, was talking to Sixto in a low voice. The slender young boy in front of him kept his eyes down as he pulled.

Driving off the ferry, Balthazar could see that the men on the shore were now dumping small blue-and-white crabs from the traps, delicately detaching those who clung to the wire with their claws. In the center of the trap a fat turkey wing dangled from a string.

Sixto said, "The Loiza police have questioned that ferryman about the body found in the cove we passed. They wanted to know who he took over that evening. But he had a lot of passengers—locals and strangers. And one can get to the road from the main highway, too. He did not want to talk. He is scared. Hard to understand, too."

"I had the same trouble with the old man. I *think* he said it was not police business because there were no wrists for handcuffs."

At the end of the street that led to the ferry stood a handsome, cream-colored Spanish-style Catholic church that faced a small paved square with benches and a few trees. The benches baking in the sun were empty, but a few older men lounged under every tree, silently watching the parade of cars that jammed the narrow one-way street around the square. Tiny shops, all in need of paint, faced three sides of the square. On the fourth side was a new sand-colored municipal building.

"This way to the police station," Sixto said, turning down a narrow street lined with buildings whose flower-filled balconies overhung it. "They are expecting us."

As they rounded a corner onto the two-lane highway that served as the main street of the town, Balthazar's attention was caught by an impossibly neat white house. It looked as if the occupants spent every waking hour on its exterior. Not even a twig littered the yard. A large sign said Hogar Crea and asked if the passer-by had the qualities of control, integrity, responsibility, and honesty, among others. Two young men, dressed completely in white, sat upright on the porch, their hands folded in their lap.

Across the street, a hodge-podge of small stores almost obscured the entrance to a large modern baseball stadium. Sixto slowed and turned into a dirt parking lot across from the stadium.

"The police station is supposed to be here." They examined the assortment of buildings.

"There," said Sixto, pointing to a large painting of the badge of the Puerto Rico police on a balcony above a mini-market with dilapidated white grillwork.

Dodging through the heavy traffic, they crossed the highway and went up the creaking wooden outside staircase, Sixto leading. The Loiza station was a large, spare, linoleum-floored room on the second floor. A thin uneven coat of beige paint covered water-stained walls. A few metal chairs were lined on one side of the room, and at the far end was a high desk on a square podium. Seated there, a black police officer who looked sixteen, glanced up from his writing as they entered. His expression when he saw their identification betrayed that he had certainly not been expecting them.

"I am Patrolman Velez," he stammered, "and Sergeant Terron is not here, unfortunately. His mother is not well, and he had to take her to the hospital in Carolina. You did not stop at the Carolina Headquarters?"

Sixto explained that they had not come on the highway, but rather across on the ferry.

"Ah." Velez was clearly wondering what to do.

"I understand that the Sergeant had arranged rooms for us at the government resort."

The young man's face brightened. "*Sí*, the *Centro Vacacional*. I will call one of the officers on duty and he can show you there and . . . explain the situation."

He got up and gestured toward the balcony overlooking the road. "Perhaps you would like to wait out there. The chairs are more comfortable. I will use the radio."

Sixto and Balthazar looked down at the narrow, crowded street. Bicyclists, pedestrians, chickens, and dogs crowded on the unpaved shoulders, darting in and out of the traffic. An old man seated on a fat donkey plodded on the edge of the pavement, oblivious to the quick cars. Many were gleaming Japanese Toyota Corollas, looking like small boys' models. Their regular tires had been replaced by little ones, and their frames almost scraped the ground.

In the background, they could hear Velez repeating call numbers.

Balthazar pointed at the well-kept white house. "What's Hogar Crea?"

"Drug rehabilitation center," Sixto replied. "They have them in several places around the island. For young men. They're pretty successful, but the drug problem in Puerto Rico is very bad."

The policeman's voice reciting the numbers became increasingly more insistent. Balthazar strolled inside and pretended to be studying the large organizational chart of the station, hanging across the room from the podium. It was printed but the writing in the neat boxes containing the names of the local men had long ago faded. Someone had scrawled an obscenity, in Spanish and English, on one corner in red ink.

Finally he turned to the desk. He waited until

Velez paused, microphone in hand, and said, "There's no need to disturb your men if they're busy. It's nearly five; why don't you just point us in the direction of the Center?"

"No one seems to be near their radios—" Velez stopped, realizing too late that he'd said the wrong thing. "It's almost the dinner hour," he went on, making things worse. His misery increased.

"Speaking of dinner," Balthazar interjected pleasantly, pretending to overlook Velez's discomfiture, "I'd like to try some crab. Where could we eat?"

Hurriedly, the patrolman sketched the route to the resort, adding that the restaurant there was probably not open now. He drew a quick sketch of another road and marked the Restaurante Rosado. "Very good crab there," he assured Balthazar. They thanked him and left.

The traffic thinned slightly as they passed a cemetery with high white stone walls. Through the padlocked wrought-iron gates, Balthazar glimpsed the flower-bedecked, crowded graves, some with tall crosses and statues of angels. Every space in the large cemetery seemed occupied, but the pedestrians, recklessly scampering back and forth across the street, heedless of the traffic, seemed anxious to join their ancestors there. The owner of every house, shack, market, and outdoor bar had apparently been determined to build as close as possible to the little two-lane road, and clusters of people, young and old, almost all black, stood chatting everywhere, sometimes on the highway itself. There was a slight haze, and the smell of wood-smoke and cooking food filled the soft air.

"You know, Sixto, when I first arrived, I was amused because the people in San Juan referred to everything outside of the city as *en la isla*—out on the island. As if it were a different world. But this is."

"*Sí*," Sixto said, worriedly running his fingers through his hair as a thin boy ran inches away from the Nova. "I wonder about this resort. Maybe I should have taken Mama's advice and tied a mattress to the top of the car."

They passed large palm fields dotted with grazing black and white cows. Then they saw the large square pillars that announced in curved script: *Centro Vacacional U.I.A.* An attractive sign advertised the restaurant and gave the chef's name. The winding gravel driveway into the grounds was beautifully landscaped. There was an enormous lagoon on one side, with ducks and swans placidly swimming in the still green water. On the east side of the drive, a high chain-link fence was bordered with lush plants and topped with flowering fuchsia bougainvillea. They stopped as the fence crossed the drive next to a one-room building with large glass windows. Through the gate they could see an Olympic-sized pool, glinting in the early evening sun. Beyond that stretched rows of attractive, two-story buildings facing the drive, their backs to the lagoon.

The small office seemed empty and the gate seemed locked.

A handsome young man, who looked more European than Puerto Rican, hurried around the corner, tugging on the gold chain around his neck. He leaned down to the car, smiled, and said in unaccented English, "You're the officers from San Juan? Just let me open the gate and get your keys. Then I'll drive with you to your unit and make sure it's ready. And, before I forget," his smile grew wider, "a Señora Cardenas called." He looked at Sixto. "Your mom?"

Sixto nodded resignedly.

"She's left a message. She says that Cousin Ida brought you a cream-cheese flan right after you left. But your Uncle Pepe is going to Fajardo tomorrow and he'll drop it off. I'll put it in your refrigerator."

He disappeared into the building, leaving behind him the pleasant scent of piney aftershave, and the gate slid open noiselessly. He returned and climbed into the back seat of the car with a bunch of keys in one hand and a can of cockroach spray in the other. The gate shut behind them as they continued down the long drive.

"It's not an electric eye. You have to honk when you want in or out. But it works with a key, too. I can give you one since you're our only guests. Pretty quiet here in the winter," he continued chattily, "but we did have a few people over the weekend. That's why I have to put you in the very last unit down near the convention center and the ocean. That building should be cleaned now. The painters are working on some of the others. Go all the way to the end of the drive."

Hopping out of the car, he went ahead of them into a downstairs unit. There was a narrow corridor with a bath on one side and a small built-in kitchen on the other. As he walked through, he brushed the walls, removing small dried husks. "Lizard droppings," he explained. "No problem." Flipping on the bathroom light, he scrutinized the immaculate white-tiled room. Leaning over, he sprayed a heavy mist of insecticide at every corner of the shower. He stepped back, filled the room with spray and then firmly closed the door. Sixto coughed, clapped his hand over his mouth, pointed to the trunk of the car, and disappeared to get the luggage.

"The kitchens and the bath are in front," their host continued, "so all the patios and balconies overlook the lagoon. But don't worry, they spray a lot. Keeps the mosquitoes down. Still, you have to keep the screens closed. Or you can leave these windows closed and just turn on the air conditioning. Nice breezes here, now, though."

As he talked, he continued to spray. There was a stripped double bed in the center of the room, and a small table with two chairs with rusted legs. He opened the other door, revealing a smaller room with a bed pushed against a big window. He sprayed that room thoroughly, too.

"Looks okay," he nodded at last, apparently unaffected by the pervasive chemical mist. "I have the maids start at the end while the families are still moving out in the morning. That way the women don't complain. For the last few months, they haven't wanted to work in this building if it's empty, even two at a time."

"Why not?" Balthazar asked, trying not to breathe. "Are they bothered by the stories of the bodies on the beach?"

"Well, that." The young man answered, now shooting the noxious spray around the modern little kitchen unit. "But a couple of them swear they've seen a Taino Indian wandering around early in the morning. A ghost. In the daytime. In the kitchen of the convention hall."

He rolled his eyes. "In Hotel/Restaurant School they don't tell you half about the problems you're going to have with help. Even the security guard that does the rounds at night. . . . He swears he's seen the ghost too. Trying to get into the building. At least he didn't tell me the guy walked through a wall."

He peered into the refrigerator. "There's some ice, but I can sell you some, too. Big freezer chest in the office. And a pay phone. No phones in the rooms, but I take messages. You did bring sheets and towels? Good. Anything else?"

"Can you get to the beach or is it fenced off?" Balthazar asked.

"Well, there's a gate, but it's always kept locked. We can't be responsible for guests out there—kids, you know. And there's quite an undertow and big waves this time of year. Besides, there's a drop-off below the gate. You have to climb down the rocks."

"I like to swim in the morning. Is there any chance I could get a key?"

"Oh, the pool's ready. Of course we don't have a lifeguard now."

"I'd like to swim in the ocean."

"Really?" The young man paused, then took two keys off the ring in his hand. "This'll open the padlock. And this opens the driveway gate. Of course, there's always someone here at night, but the guard has to check the buildings. If you're late, you might have to wait quite a while until he gets back. I guess I can trust the police with the keys." His smile was charming. "My name is Pierre. Let me know if you need anything." He trotted off.

Sixto hurried in with the last box, shoved it on top of the stove, and he and Balthazar raced together to the windows and sliding doors to the patio and threw them open. They inhaled the fresh air gratefully.

"That stuff must kill cockroaches," Balthazar said. "It just about finished me off. Let's unload the car and go eat while this place airs out."

9

THE RESTAURANTE ROSADO was unpretentious, despite the large signs advertising lobster, live crab, shrimp and red snapper. It was attached to a rather ramshackle filling station. The graveled parking area in front was filled with cars.

The interior was spacious and high-ceilinged. Slowly rotating overhead fans stirred the rich odors wafting from the kitchen. It was very crowded.

A plump, attractive woman in her mid-forties slipped around the end of the bar and walked, smiling, toward Balthazar and Sixto. She wore a soft, loose shirt covered with bright gold sequins, matching trousers tight at the ankles, and very high-heeled white sandals. Enormous gold hoop earrings dangled from her ears, and her arms were adorned with shining bangles. She was heavily made-up, and she had the assured air of a woman who has always been attractive to men.

"Good evening. The officers from San Juan, no? Come to eat the crab?" Her English was unaccented but had a musical Spanish lilt. Without waiting for them to answer, she nodded and went on. "Good. I'm Panama." She shook hands lightly with both men and beckoned them to follow her. "Plenty of room in back and on the other side."

All the people seated at the long mahogany bar either turned and stared at the officers or eyed them covertly in the mirrored tiles above the bar. Most of the tables were occupied by large families. The children gaped unabashedly at them; the parents unsuccessfully tried to avoid giving the impression of doing so.

One enormous black man seated at the end of the bar, head slumped forward, lifted his head and stared groggily at Balthazar. He squinted and said, as if it were a greeting, "Nebraska!"

"Ah, no," Balthazar replied. "*Nueva* York."

The man abruptly grabbed the detective's arm and repeated "*Nueva* York" dazedly. Then he focused his eyes, and let go. "*Lajara*," he spat out, and turned away.

"*Lajara?*" Balthazar asked when he caught up with Panama. "What does that mean?"

She half-shrugged. "When the Puerto Ricans first went to New York, a lot of the police were Irish, and a lot of them were named O'Hara. The Puerto Ricans couldn't say it right. They still call them *lajaras*."

The large room was divided by a half-wall topped by white wrought iron. Thick vines of tropical plants covered the grillwork, effectively separating the two areas. As they walked through the door in the back, the woman gestured to a large dark area covered with wood slats and wire mesh in the corner. "You can pick out your own crabs."

She clicked on an overhead light. Under the mesh, the crabs scuttled clumsily sideways in the crowded pit, their armored bodies clattering together and against the shallow metal dishes filled with water and corn. Their bodies were baseball-sized and bright blue, their spider-like legs fat. From their slanted eyesockets protruded pea-sized eyes on thin tendrils, eyes which seemed to stare upwards unblinkingly and aggressively, even as they tried to edge toward the darker corners.

Both men started slightly, and Panama giggled. "Evil-looking, no? Land crabs, not sea crabs. They live in the mountains. Good to eat. I'll show you how."

She turned to the twelve empty tables scattered around the inner room. "Sit over by the window. It's a little quieter back there. All my customers like that damned jukebox. Now then: rum, beer, or whisky?" Without pausing, she went on. "No, not much whisky.

Bunch of the young blacks in here late last night—
estúpidos—all ordering Scotch to impress their girlfriends.
Have rum with soda." Without waiting for an answer
she returned to the bar.

The large windows around the room were covered
with decorative ironwork and screens instead of glass.
Stretched out on the inside of the screen next to their
table was a little brown lizard, its dainty feet splayed
against the wire. Its snakelike head was lifted alertly,
but it remained frozen on the screen, its eyes seemingly
focused in an unconcerned manner somewhere over their
shoulders. But as they moved their chairs, it darted
swiftly to the rafters of the room, which were overlaid
with thick straw. Its movement sent another delicate
lizard scurrying toward the cover of the plants.

Panama returned, setting down their glasses. "*Tostones*
or french fries? *Tostones*—much better with the crab,"
she answered herself, shaking her damp hands to dry
them. "Rice comes with the meal. It'll take awhile.
There's only the cook and one waiter. Have to do every
damned thing myself. I'll send over your salad. You're
lucky. I have a ripe avocado."

Just then they heard a loud rustle overhead. They
looked up to see a flash of brown and a long, fat tail.
"Big lizard," Balthazar remarked in surprise.

"No." Panama shook her head at his naiveté. "A rat.
They live in the palm trees here, eat the coconuts.
Don't come down to the ground much. You can't catch
the damned things. But you have to watch them, keep
the crabs covered. They like the crabs. In the mountains the rats catch them and eat them. Takes the rats
awhile, but they're faster than the crabs. Pretty soon,
the rat bites off the crab's eyes. Then the crab is helpless. The rat has sharp, sharp teeth. Bites off the crab's
legs. Eats them one at a time. I'll send the waiter over."
Her bracelets jingled musically as she walked.

Balthazar and Sixto regarded each other in silence.
They sipped their drinks.

"Have you ever seen crabs like that, Sixto?"

"No," said Sixto, "never."

A waiter wearing thick glasses that rode on the tip of his nose came up carrying an enormous white plastic bucket. His hair was curly, but thinning. It stuck straight up from his forehead, giving the impression he was endlessly surprised. "Come," he said breathlessly, "pick out your crabs."

He turned on the light, chuckling as the crabs scuttled. "They no like the light." He shoved back the top and reached down with a large pair of tongs. "Here's a good one—female. Lots of good eggs inside. You need about six each."

"That's a lot," Balthazar began, "maybe . . ."

"Not that much meat. Many, many people eat twelve," the waiter declared. He lifted each squirming crab up for inspection and then thrust it into the pail. Smiling somewhat fatuously, he hurried away.

Balthazar and Sixto looked through the screen door at the enormous back area. There were three large outdoor party pavilions, with white wrought-iron sides and heavy straw roofs. The pavilions were filled with metal folding chairs and long tables. At the very end of the last one, an old man sat on the ground, huddled over a plate of food. His donkey grazed quietly beside him.

Panama came up behind them. "Just had the pavilions repainted," she said cheerfully. "Looks nice, no? I have five hundred people sometimes. Wedding dinners, holidays. But the damned painters tried to overcharge me. Bunch of jerks. They think because I'm a woman alone I don't know what things cost. Just a minute. The old man out there has got some of my knives. Resharpening them. He's so crazy, he might go off and forget to give them back to me." She hurried through the door, leaving behind a generous cloud of perfume.

Balthazar stood and wandered around the room, looking at the paintings hanging between the wall openings. There were several unframed ones all clearly done by the same local artist: one sketch of the ferry boat, one of a pile of malevolent-looking blue crabs, and a startlingly detailed one of a devil's mask with blank, black eyeholes and curving fangs. On the largest wall was an oil painting covered with glass and mounted in an ornate wooden frame. It was a nineteenth-century work depicting a child's funeral in the tropics. Various mourning relatives, all blacks, solemnly encircled a tiny lace-covered coffin. In the shadowed corner were two white priests in cassocks looking joyously up to the heavens. Directly in front of the coffin, his sad eyes on the ground, stood a witch doctor, wearing heavy necklaces of seashells, feathers, and golden amulets, clutching a beaded rattle.

Balthazar turned back to the table and found his way blocked by the drunken black man from the bar. In his hand gleamed a long, curved machete. "Nicaragua," he said, sneering.

Stepping back instinctively, Balthazar grabbed a chair and raised it. The drunk grinned, swung his weapon high above his head and crashed it down on the chair legs, slicing them off cleanly. "*Lajara*," he said, grunting with satisfaction.

Balthazar whacked him in the stomach with the side of the chair just as Sixto vaulted over a table and onto the man's back. The machete clattered to the floor, and the man lurched through the screen door at the back, screeching incomprehensibly.

Once outside, he stumbled forward and sprawled heavily on the grass by the door, Sixto still clinging to his shoulders. Panama shrieked and came running forward on her high heels. The old man to whom she had been talking looked up in fright, dropped his dish and ran for his donkey. He scrambled onto its back and rode off hastily.

Balthazar slammed through the door and put his pistol to the fallen man's temple. Sixto pulled back his unresisting arms and yanked out his handcuffs.

"Wait, wait." Panama reached them, panting, one shoe off. "There is no need," she said, pushing at Sixto. "Move your gun," she ordered Balthazar. He stepped back slightly, warily, the gun still outstretched.

With her one shod foot, Panama began kicking the

fallen man's ribs. He rolled over, groaned, stood up shakily, and backed away from her, arms raised to protect his face.

"Pablo, you *estúpido!*" she screamed at him, and then began a colorful outpouring of Spanish invective. She told him his head was empty and graphically described how defective other parts of his body were. He slunk backwards down the path to the pavilion. She was slapping at his upraised arms, her bracelets clashing as she struck him. Finally, she yanked off her other shoe, and began beating him with that. He stopped, hangdog, head bent forward, arms lowered, against the grillwork of the pavilion.

Panama pulled a key from her bra, and opened the padlock of the pavilion with a jerk. She pushed him in and he fell backward against a long table. She never stopped berating him, his parents, his grandparents, and his great-grandparents. He climbed up on the table, and turning away from her, lay down and put his fingers in his ears.

She turned, slammed the wrought-iron door, and padlocked it. Slipping her shoe back on, she went in search of the other. As she walked back toward the two detectives, she was tugging down her shirt and rearranging her bracelets. "Stupid jerk," she panted. "I'm sorry. Pablo's usually no trouble. But the waiter probably let him have another drink when I was back with the cook."

Holding onto Balthazar's shoulder, she brushed off the bottom of her foot and replaced her other stiletto-heeled shoe. "I didn't notice he'd brought his machete in—he's been opening coconuts for me outside. He'll be all right in there until morning. His brother was killed in New York—by a cop. Better off—he was even stupider than Pablo. But maybe you won't cause trouble for him? I'll explain to Sergeant Terron."

She pulled open the screen and waved the men inside. Leaning over the table she swooped up their glasses.

"Um, perhaps just soda this time," Balthazar said.

"Next one," she said without stopping. "You need another to relax. The drinks are on the house."

The waiter entered carrying a tray with two bowls overflowing with crisp lettuce, slices of red tomato and light green avocado. He swiftly set out carafes of vinegar and oil, a large cold bottle of Thousand Island dressing, and a small wooden bread board and a thick wooden stick with rounded edges. "Crab coming," he announced and disappeared.

"When I tell Mama about those crabs—and this place—I don't think she's going to believe me."

"I don't believe you, either," Balthazar said. He looked down. He was still holding his gun. He looked around slowly, and then put it away. There was no sound from Pablo in his cage.

The waiter soon reappeared pushing a large metal trolley. An enormous pile of pale orange rice was surrounded by thick slices of golden fried plantain; two big platters were filled with boiled crab, now a rich brown color. "Panama say she come right away." He, too, dropped the endings of all his words.

"Now," Panama entered, carrying a tray with three drinks. She sat down, pulled the wooden board toward her, and took a sip out of the tallest glass. "Damned doctor said no more rum, just coco water and whisky." She pronounced it 'wicky.' "But I need it to relax. I have to get up by six to order food, and then I'm on my feet all day long."

"This is kind of you," Balthazar began, "but I know you're awfully busy now and—"

"No," Panama interrupted, "they've all gone home."

"Already? I hope we haven't chased. . . ."

"No, no, no, no," she replied, not looking at Balthazar directly, "they eat early here, go to bed early."

She picked up a crab, laid it on the board, pulled off its legs and detached the claws, which she expertly cracked with the stick. She handed one to each of them. "Very greasy crabs; you don't need butter."

Then she split open the thick body with one swift blow. "Now inside you see, lots of good eggs." She mixed a heaping spoon of rice with the thick liquid in the crab's body. "Here, try that."

"Delicious." Balthazar spoke sincerely. The claw was sweet, and the mixture in the body had a heavy, nutty flavor.

She giggled with pleasure. "People come from all over the island to eat these damned crab. When the bridge is finished a year from now I'll have even more customers. I owned a restaurant in Isla Verde a couple of years ago. I drove by here one day; this place was closed, falling down. Old man Rosado's son ran the restaurant, but he was killed. Car accident. Just a young man. He didn't do the food right—just sold a lot of beer. I grew up in Panama. My mother and her mother ran a big place there. My grandmother did really well. Of course, she kept some girls upstairs, made good money off the whores. But my mother—she was no businesswoman. I went to a restaurant school in New York."

She talked quickly, but she dissected the crabs even more quickly. "No, no, no, no," she said, reaching over and taking a large claw from Balthazar's hands. "You're not doing it right. See." She extracted the claw whole from its shell and held it out to him. "Takes some practice."

Patiently, she showed them how to get the smallest piece of meat from the legs. At last, satisfied with their skills, she leaned back and sipped her drink.

"This town's different from San Juan, no?" she asked, smiling at Sixto.

Sixto nodded, his mouth full of crab.

"Now tomorrow at breakfast, you'll meet here the mayors of Loiza and Rio Grande." She jerked her head to indicate the small town to the south. "I told them nine o'clock. They'll be late. That way you can have coffee with Sergeant Terron first. He'll stop by here sometime tonight on his way back from the hospital. I'll tell him."

She roared with laughter at their surprised looks. "Oh *sí, sí.* This is a small town. Everybody comes here. Where else they going to go? Five minutes after you left the Ancon, everybody in town knew of your arrival. So the mayor—I mean the one from Loiza, Couvertier's his name—gets right on the phone. Says he wants to meet with you. Says to call up Mayor Montanez from Rio Grande. Now Montanez—he's all right. But Mayor Couvertier, he's a *cangriman*!" There was sarcasm in her voice, but she winked at Sixto.

"A *cangriman*?" Balthazar asked.

"You know," she said, "thinks he's a big shot. When the Puerto Ricans went to America, they couldn't pronounce 'congressman.' A *cangriman* is someone who thinks he's very, very important. Couvertier's got the big idea that he's going to make Loiza a tourist center." Her laughter was young and infectious.

"Hm," Sixto relinquished a crab leg he'd been sucking enthusiastically. "But even when the bridge is finished, it'll be a long time before that road is ready."

"*Sí, sí.* They say three years, but you know Puerto Rico. People move a lot slower here than they do in Panama. But still, when Loiza is ten minutes from Isla Verde instead of half an hour many people will move here."

"Running this place you must hear a lot," Balthazar said. "What do the local people say about the bodies on the beach?"

"Nothing," she said.

"Nothing?"

She shrugged. "They shut up, change the subject. They don't say anything in front of me. But down in all those little shacks they call bars, they talk. But not to the police, no. I tell you what, you talk to the Americans who live on the beach."

"The Americans?"

"Well, the *Norteamericanos*. They're friends of mine. Josh and Felicity Sterling. Very famous, you know, and rich. They live in *Playa del Mar*. It's a development down from the *Centro Vacacional*. They live right on the beach. Every winter they come here."

She got up and returned with the bill. "I gave you a good price on the crab. In the winter they're scarcer.

Sometimes the old men in the mountains charge me $5.00 each. Damned peasants."

As they left the now nearly empty restaurant, she called after them. "I have a good ham—Oscar Mayer. Ham and cheese omelet for breakfast."

10

THE SUN HAD ALREADY SET. The mountains to the south, which had looked green and empty during the day, were now spangled with hundreds of lights. They contrasted with *El Yunque* and its surrounding hills, which were shrouded in darkness.

To the east, San Juan threw brightness at the sky, but even the city lights looked dim next to the radiance of an almost full moon, climbing the sky. It gave the few fluffy clouds remaining a daylight whiteness.

"Good time to take a look at that beach. Good light. . . . Maybe we'll spot the body-dumper," Balthazar said.

"We could then go back to San Juan tomorrow," Sixto answered wistfully. He paused and looked over his shoulder. "But of course, there are still many, many uneaten crabs in that restaurant."

Although it was early in the evening, there was only an occasional pedestrian and very little traffic along the two miles to the government resort. And when they arrived at its interior gate, the small office was dark.

"Good thing we have a key. Guard must be doing early rounds," Balthazar said. "Let's park down by the convention center. We can just leave our shoes in the car, take the flashlight, and climb down those rocks to the beach."

They unstrapped their guns from their ankles, tucked them into their belts, rolled up their pants, and headed for the back gate.

The young manager of the resort had not exaggerated the steepness of the rocky climb down to the beach, but the moon's brilliance made the flashlight unnecessary. Balthazar was surprised at how little his knee bothered him. He felt the stirrings of eagerness which always signaled the beginning of a case. There was even an air of truancy about their endeavors. And the smell and sound of the sea brought back sharp memories of summer camp. Balthazar's Aunt Gretje, who had raised him, had been a firm believer in the wisdom of putting boys in touch with nature.

The warm seafoam curled around their feet. They stood on the beach, silent before its perfect beauty. The tide was high, the white sand gleamed and the crests of the crashing waves were whiter than the moon. Dark palms and soft, long-needled pine trees lined the beach.

A mile away, the high, tree-covered promontory marking the mouth of the Loiza River cut off the glare of San Juan. To the east, the warm orange of a few sodium vapor streetlights were visible. The lights of a few small fishing boats flickered on the horizon. But the beach and the sea were empty.

"If we had just a short tower—and the right kind of eyes—I bet we could see clear to Spain on a night like this." Balthazar sighed. "I'd give a lot of dollars to live on a beach like this. And speaking of that, what kind of possible profit could there be in cluttering up this beach with dead bodies?"

"You could scare people away at night that way. Then," Sixto eyed the faraway boats, "that could make smuggling easier."

"Possible," Balthazar agreed. "What are they bringing ashore? Haitian immigrants?"

"It's possible." Sixto traced a line in the sand with his toe. "Instead of trying to land them in Miami, you bring them back here. Some might have relatives in this town. Eventually, they could find their way to the United States. But there is a problem. No one can make money off the Haitians. They have no money."

"How likely a spot for drug smuggling would this

be?" Balthazar looked out and saw no waves breaking except at the shore. "I see a second line of white caps some distance from the shore down there past Loiza—probably means reefs—but there don't seem to be any right here."

Sixto nodded. "But the drug smugglers have the best boats—big and fast. How big a boat could come ashore here, especially at night?"

"Good question. Sergeant Terron may have already looked into that. But if the Drug Enforcement Agency is stepping up its efforts on the Florida coast, the shippers from South America could use this as a switching point instead. We're less than five hundred miles from some of their big ports. Think about the advantages of an isolated beach right next to a population center the size of San Juan."

They walked on in silence. At last Balthazar said, "Even though the highway is jammed with cars and the other route almost impassable, I'm still surprised that more people don't live here. So far I've only glimpsed three houses near the beach. If they are houses. There are no lights. Of course, there could be a lot more huts back in the fields, but the only sign of people are these wide tracks from dune buggies."

"*Mira*," Sixto exclaimed suddenly. "Maybe not *drugs*. The people here are not rich. They could make money just bringing in liquor. St. Thomas is only a short distance from here. Scotch there is a third of the price, and cigarettes half as cheap. The boat would not have to be so large."

"That's an idea. The highways between North Carolina and New York are crowded with trucks bringing in the cheaper cigarettes illegally. Same federal tax but a big difference in the two states' taxes. Why not here? We'll run it by Terron tomorrow." He paused. "Or should we? Local police would likely be cut in on that kind of operation."

Sixto did not reply.

Stopping again to gaze at the way the ocean, too, was the color of liquid moon, Balthazar drank in the sweet, silent air. He remembered how excitedly his young wife Rose would pack up for a day at Jones Beach at the first sign of a weak spring sun. She never swam, preferring just to loll and doze on a beach towel, as she said, "like an enchanted white slug, toasting near the sea." He closed his eyes against the inner sight of her. The memory of the cold months following her death caused him to shiver in the warm air.

"Help!" Sixto called. He'd waded out and was pulling in a huge driftwood log. Balthazar rolled his pants up higher and dashed into the surf. As they tugged on its weight, Balthazar thought of a bonfire on the beach, the flames flickering on Maira Knight's ivory skin, on a glass of clear white wine in her slender fingers, reflecting in her light eyes. She said she loved to swim. He would bring her here.

Straining and grunting, the two men heaved the tree trunk from the sea and dragged it high on the shore. Grinning with mutual satisfaction, they dusted the sand from their hands. As they turned back, Balthazar found himself yawning hugely although it was only nine o'clock.

Back at their unit, Sixto unlocked the door, switched on the light, then lunged forward suddenly. Balthazar reached for his gun and then saw the reason for Sixto's hurry.

The hallway walls, the cabinets of the kitchenette, and the floor were alive with scuttling brown cockroaches.

Sixto turned, then raised an eyebrow at the sight of the gun. "Here," he said, thrusting a folded copy of a magazine into Balthazar's hand. "Don't shoot them—we have not that many bullets."

They swatted vigorously, then turned on the bathroom lights and started in there. Balthazar turned to see one huge cockroach, half the size of a mouse, scurrying toward the closet door. He hit it repeatedly.

"I think the spray slows them down," Sixto said, panting.

Balthazar looked down at the squashed cockroach. "Maybe, but it doesn't inhibit their growth. Here in

Loiza, you don't have to get in touch with nature; it keeps getting in touch with you."

In the middle of the night, Balthazar suddenly found himself awake. He listened intently, trying to identify the sound that had alarmed him. He heard only the whirr of the insects, the occasional queries of the tree frogs, the swish and roar of the nearby sea.

Then to his surprise, it struck him that it was a smell that had awakened him—an overpowering smell. His bed in the smaller room was directly under a large screened area. Someone was standing there. The odor was unmistakable. It was the pungent, almost acrid, stink of an unwashed human being. One wearing musty clothing. The clothing, he thought, smelled as if it were even rotting, as though it had been buried, not exposed to air.

He remained frozen. If the man were that close, surely any movement could be heard. But how could anyone get over those high gates? He heard the soft scrabble of fingers brushing across the screen, fingers feeling blindly. He realized with discomfort that he could not hear the sound of anyone breathing, however lightly.

He reached slowly and carefully for his gun on the bedside table. A bedspring creaked slightly. The sound of exploring fingers ceased abruptly. And then Balthazar heard the jingle of what sounded like keys.

He relaxed a little. The security guard, probably, although even if he did work alone, somebody should advise the guy to take an occasional shower. It was odd, though, to be awakened by an odor. Still, the smell of smoke woke people in burning buildings, and man must once have relied on his sense of smell to keep from danger.

He heard another noise. Someone was quietly prying at the edge of the light aluminum screen. That *wasn't* the guard. Silently, he slid out of bed and opened the connecting door.

Creeping to the narrow bed, he put his hand on Sixto's shoulder and his mouth against his ear. He felt the young man's quick start to instant wakefulness. "Be quiet," he whispered urgently. "Someone's outside on the patio. Get your gun and the flashlight. We'll go out the front."

At the door, Balthazar murmured, "You go right, I'll go left. When I yell, turn on the light." The wooden door opened noiselessly, but the metal screen door made a scraping noise. They waited a few seconds, then Sixto slipped off into the shadows to the right and Balthazar, feeling his way by touching the brick wall lightly, went to the left.

He turned the first corner and walked into a wall of mosquitoes. They not only covered the naked upper half of his body, but clung to his legs, his ankles, even his toes. The urge to slap, brush, scratch was almost irresistible. He clenched his teeth, cursing the nearness of the lagoon which must be their breeding ground. He recalled, too, that the map had shown a good-sized lake east of the resort. He went on, footstep by footstep, over the uneven ground.

The moon had disappeared behind the thick trees on the far side of the lagoon and the darkness was absolute. But there were the outside lights of the distant resort office to the south. Would he be outlined, however dimly, as he rounded the corner? He crouched down, put both hands on the gun and leaned his head around the corner.

He looked straight down toward the far corner where Sixto would be and could catch no movement at all. He tried to remember whether there were bushes on that corner.

Swiveling, he made out a dark shape next to the thick trunks of the trees near the water. He straightened a little and immediately heard a sharp whine and, right above his head, a rush of air. Metal clanged hollowly on the iron railing of the balcony above. "Now!" he yelled, gripping his gun tightly.

Sixto's flashlight caught the heavy metal weight,

still swinging from the railing. It looked suspended in mid-air, held by nothing at all. There was a loud splash in the lagoon and the sudden terrified squawks of the disturbed water fowl. The flashlight whirled, bobbing as Sixto ran toward the water.

In the light's darting beam, the complaining birds swam, flew, and skittered across the ruffled surface of the lagoon. Sixto swung the flashlight in a wide arc, but there was so much movement, it was impossible to focus on any one spot. Panting, the two men stood, desperately trying to pierce the darkness, staring intently down at the water. The birds, upset by the intruding light, fluttered in every direction to avoid its glare.

Sixto wove the flashlight in and out of the tall reeds and thick leaves of the water lilies that lined the shores. Startled frogs jumped and heavy-bodied insects rose in panicked flight. Both men constantly and unconsciously scraped the mosquitoes away. "Six poachers," Balthazar hissed furiously, "and a small guerilla army could be in that water, breathing through reeds or whatever the hell they do."

Sixto turned the flashlight back at the building. "It's a fishing line," he said. The gray hunk of lead swayed, pendulum like. As they moved closer, they could just make out the colorless nylon thread to which it was attached.

Balthazar thought of the speed and force that the fisherman in the cove had used to throw his weight out into the sea. "If someone caught you around the neck with that, you'd stop breathing."

"It would not break," Sixto agreed, tugging futilely at the line entangled in the open grillwork of the railing. "Someone could have thought the resort was empty, tried to catch a fat duck, wrap the line around its neck? Or you think . . . our necks?"

"Whoever it was, and I do not think that the ghosts of the Tainos still fish, could at least see better in the dark than we can. Also, he must have mosquito repellent on. He's gone. Let's go in. Either the security guard is

sleeping pretty soundly, or else he thinks we're engag-
ing in night maneuvers."

Reluctantly, after checking the screens and the lock
on the patio door, Balthazar went back to bed.

The next noise he heard was Sixto tapping gently
on the door. "It's almost eight. We overslept."

As they headed toward the gate, it slid open across
the driveway. Pierre's cheerful face appeared at the
window of the office. "Keep the key, will you?" he said.
"Glad I gave it to you last night. I would have had to
come back and let you in. Guard called in sick." He
waved them on with a smile.

11

THE UNIFORMED POLICEMAN sitting with Panama rose
as they entered the restaurant. If the reports had not
noted Sergeant Terron's thirty years in the *Policia*,
Balthazar would have thought him a much younger
man. His black face was unlined, his carriage erect, his
physique solid. Balthazar had often been impressed with
the fact that most of the Puerto Rican police seemed in
excellent physical shape.

"Terron," the officer said briefly. "Glad you're
here." As they shook hands, Balthazar noticed the faint
droop in the man's left eyelid. When Terron turned
then to grasp Sixto's hand with only that side of his
face visible, Balthazar had the vivid impression that the
two sides of his face were mismatched. The left seemed
sinister.

Panama scrambled to her feet. She was carefully
made-up and dressed in a neat, pale blue pants suit.
"Fresh coffee in a minute," she promised, and moved off
to the kitchen.

"Sorry about the trouble here last night," the Loiza
officer said. "I'll see that it doesn't happen again. Surprised me—wouldn't have thought Pablo'd get excited,
even if he was drunk."

"You don't think anyone . . . suggested it to him?
Someone connected with the body-dumping case?"

Terron raised an eyebrow. "Doubt that Pablo'd be
able to remember what he was supposed to do. Or to
who." He frowned. "Doesn't seem likely. Out here,

you know, we don't see the kind of problems that in a big city—New York, San Juan—you might find common. An open attack on the police. A planned one. No."

Balthazar decided against mentioning the ghostly fisherman. "It's just that this is an unusual case," he said instead. "At the moment I don't see what we can do that you haven't done." He had found that approach useful. Given such an opening, most people rushed in, explaining what they had done, repeating information already given, sometimes amplifying.

Terron said nothing at all. He sat quietly, his big hands clasped around his coffee mug. Behind his almost disinterested attitude, Balthazar sensed a guarded frontier. Was Terron going to be overtly hostile or just uncooperative?

Balthazar began again. "You know this area and the people so well. What kind of explanations have you heard?"

Panama bustled in with an uncovered, steaming silver coffee pot, a small pitcher of hot milk, and two cups. Setting down the cups, she filled them with almost equal portions of both liquids. While she refilled Terron's cup, Balthazar caught a swift, undecipherable exchange of glances between the two. She hurried back into the kitchen.

Terron shrugged. "Everybody's got a different one. Depends on how it affects them personally. Be better if we could give them an official one. They wouldn't believe it. But it'd give them something to make fun of, argue with. As it is, they don't say anything much. Scares them, of course."

"Your reports indicate no sign of any unusual coastal activity. Given the length of the beaches here, I can see that it would be impossible to patrol the area adequately. Would people who live in the area report anything out of the ordinary?"

"Depends on who saw it and what they saw. This case's been going on for six months. Over the next six months, we'll hear this and that and we'll know something about it. On the other hand, if we never find another body, we'll probably never find out."

"How large a boat could you unload along here? Twenty-five-foot craft? Thirty-foot?"

"Hard to say." Terron rubbed his chin. "A man who knows what he's doing, has good charts, sticks pretty close to the mouth of the Loiza River, daylight. I'd guess so. But at night, no moon." He shook his head skeptically.

"I called the U.S. Drug boys in San Juan," he went on. "Explained. Asked them if they caught any noise about action down here. Talked a long time. They ask more questions than they answer. Wanted to know all about air strips here. Cautioned me not to do anything without checking with them first. Finally they allowed that boats might be possible. Coast Guard would take a look."

"Do many of the local residents have boats?"

"People who live here? No. Most of the people here are old and poor. Oh, some rowboats, a few outboards. Some people here fish—for their families. But most do it from the shore. Throw out fishing lines or nets. Lot of fish out there, of course."

"But no commercial fishing?"

"No place to sell the fish," Terron replied brusquely. "Some good-sized commercial fishing around the south side of the island near Ponce. Refrigerated trucks go over the mountains—hour and a half to San Juan. Take them to the hotels and big restaurants. But here, well, you could sell a few in the native markets in Rio Grande or Canovanas and a few people do, but you can't make much money. Ask Panama. Certain days, she's expecting the right crowd, she buys fresh shrimp and lobster but everything else, mostly frozen. Fry it up—most people like it, can't tell the difference. At home, most people eat salted fish—comes in from the Dominican Republic, cheap. No minimum wage there."

"People around here eat *salted* fish?"

"Sure. Mostly they just eat rice and beans every day. Kill a chicken, throw that in with the rice. Or they throw the salted fish in with the rice. Don't have stoves, refrigerators. Build a fire, heat up the rice and beans. Like I said, people here are poor."

"What about smuggling of some kind? Say, on a small scale. Liquor and cigarettes from the American Virgins?"

"Doubt it. And we'd hear about it the second time they tried it. Too many people involved. You'd have to sell it to all the small bar and market owners. Not much profit there anyway. Say they were faking government stamps on the stuff and peddling it in San Juan. Regular rounds." He glanced at Sixto. "Some store owners there'd take cheaper liquor and cigarettes even without stamps, I suppose?"

Sixto nodded, but he added, "They'd have to sell a lot to make much money."

"I can see that," Balthazar agreed. "Without stamps, the price would have to be considerably under wholesale."

"It'd mean either good-sized boats or a lot of shipments. Big trucks. Can't imagine we wouldn't hear about that. Probably," he smiled slightly, revealing a gold-capped tooth, "the next day. Small town."

"Any sign of locals involved with drug smuggling?" Balthazar asked, picking up his cup. The coffee was superb.

Terron shook his head. "Nobody being free with their change. And that'd be the first thing they'd do. It'd call for a more organized bunch than we got here. Haven't been any strangers around for any length of time."

"I noticed your drug rehabilitation center here. Aren't those young men mostly from out of town? I don't think they actually mix with the people in Loiza much either, do they?"

Terron was clearly shaken. "You mean run drugs while pretending to be a rehab center? Hogar Crea is a well-known, respected outfit. I . . . well, they're well-inspected, too." He rubbed his chin again, this time much harder. "Nothing much would surprise me, but that would. Still, you think about it. Say a couple of smart men, careful, disciplined, taking their time to get it set up right."

"Of course," Balthazar pointed out, "we're starting with the idea that the corpses are meant to keep people off the beach at night. You agree that this body-dumping would be effective?"

"That's what's bothered me all along," Terron admitted reluctantly. "Nobody goes out on the beach at night anyway. They think it's dangerous."

"Why?"

"Couple of things. Six miles of these beaches. You only see a very few expensive houses. Too isolated down here. Easy to break into no matter how much wrought iron you put up—or burglar alarms you install, either. People with money here—they live up in the mountains. You go up there, you see rows of nice houses. But not on the beach. Here only poor people live on the beach. Can't afford anything else. True all around the island—except for San Juan. There all the rich people are on the beach. Big buildings. Fancy houses."

"That's true in the States, too," Balthazar observed. "Any good beach front property is high-priced."

"Then there's the danger of hurricanes, too," Terron added, "although they're rare. Last big one thirty years ago. But you still see what's left of some solid houses, and one big restaurant."

"Those are good reasons for not building there, I can see," Balthazar commented, "but would that bother people who live around here and just wanted to walk in the moonlight, for example? We didn't see anyone on the beach last night. Are the townspeople worried about being mugged?"

"No, don't think so." Terron shook his head. "We don't have much of that. But all their lives they've heard it's dangerous to be out after dark. Can't know what's out there, they say. Superstitious bunch."

"Who owns most of the beach front property?"

"Lots of people, bits and pieces. Couple big owners. Some squatters, I suppose. As long as I can remember, the deDiego family owned a lot of acres in Rio

Grande. Daughter-in-law lives there now—she has to be in her late sixties. Kind of crazy, I hear."

He sipped his coffee. "I took a look at the property tax records a while back. Three or four corporations own some big beach front plots—never heard of their names before. Oh, and the country club people own a nice stretch."

"Country club?"

"Seawind Country Club. Fancy place between Loiza and Rio Grande. Right on the beach. Big golf course and all."

Balthazar tried and failed to imagine an elegant country club next to the ramshackle shacks he had seen so far. "Do you think most people would sell?"

"The small owners would move in a minute, you offer them anything. Most of them would rather live in town. Some of the old people just moved out there a long time ago because it was unused. They and their families been there ever since."

"You said that various people came up with different explanations for the bodies?"

"Just worried people. Most of the reasons are a little hard to believe."

"For example?"

"Oh, the funeral director's got some kind of idea that someone wants to bankrupt him. He says you could start a rumor that the bodies were really those of local townspeople. I admit that would get people here pretty excited. Then they'd use a funeral home in the next town or something. But Coret's been here for years. People trust him."

"Could bankruptcy possibly benefit him?"

Terron looked blank.

"I mean does he own the business?"

"His father owned it and left it to him."

"Were there any other heirs?"

"Couple of sisters, I guess. Don't live around here anymore."

"Suppose he has to pay part of his profits to them. This business goes bankrupt. You say the people trust him. So he starts a new business on his own. This time all the profits are his."

Terron stared at Balthazar slowly. He stood up. "I'll check on it. Wouldn't have even thought of that." He paused, "Maybe you should talk to the Americans who live in Playa del Mar."

"Panama suggested that. Do you think they might have seen something?"

Terron scowled. "They live right on the beach. Nice people. The Sterlings. I talked to them for a long time. But . . . my English isn't that good. Maybe they'll mention something to you that I missed. You've come up with some things that I guess I'd better check out. Might not be a bad idea for you to come back to the station later today. Think I'll dig out all the interviews. Didn't send them all to you." Terron put on his hat and left, looking troubled.

Two men entered the restaurant. One was quite tall, but stooped. His tightly curled graying hair encircled a high forehead; the frames of his round glasses exactly matched the color of his hair. The other was extremely short and fat. His black hair was thick around his ears and neck, but he was almost completely bald on top. His head was so rounded that it looked as if it had grown right through his hair, an impression heightened by the fact that he had five or six long strands fastidiously combed over the top. These were now plastered down with sweat, despite the coolness of the morning. He bustled quickly up to their table, smiled widely, pulled out a white handkerchief, and wiped his hand before extending it.

"Ah, the officers from San Juan," he said in English. His voice was deep. "Excuse me, in this heat, I am always wetting myself with perspiration. I am the mayor of Loiza Aldea, Jesus Couvertier." He pronounced his first name in the Spanish manner—*Hay su*—but he gave his surname a French pronunciation.

Seeing Panama, who had come out of the kitchen

and was leaning on the end of the bar, he smiled so heartily that his eyes became slits. "Ah, so beautiful as usual. . . ."

The other man introduced himself with less theatricality. "Miguel Montanez, from Rio Grande. We appreciate your help." His face reflected no particular enthusiasm.

"I understand these bodies have also been found on your beaches, Mayor Montanez," Balthazar said, motioning him to a seat.

"One only—in December. Our sanitation people complain endlessly about the amount of time they must spend cleaning up the litter on the beaches. But so far we have had only one dead man there." A faint smile briefly lighted his serious face. "But our beaches are not so . . . deserted. Seawind Country Club owns a large expanse. There's part of a subdivision that extends to the water. There is even a small group of very nice houses that belong to South American families who summer here. Our summer, that is. Their winter. These houses are not empty now, though. They have servants' quarters attached, and local people occupy them year-round and look after the main houses. Still, this case is a problem for all of us. Our people worry."

"Was the body found near one of these vacation homes?"

"No, it was on the deDiego property. A fairly big piece of land—belongs to an old family here that has now died out. All, that is, but one daughter-in-law. Poor lady. She lives there by herself. Luckily she did not stumble across the body. She is not well. Her caretaker found it."

After a very detailed discussion with Panama concerning the preparation of omelets, Couvertier rejoined them.

"I am impressed with your arrival, gentlemen. Many times, I have spoken to the police here regarding their lack of punctuality in chasing this case. The people are naturally in a state of much urgency. Now Terron is a good man, but the causes here are not within his scopes."

Balthazar was completely confused, but he nodded soberly. He glanced at both Sixto and Montanez. Their faces were expressionless.

"Now," the petite Loiza mayor continued, "I have told them the causes, their understandings are not . . . are not. . . ." He struggled for the word he wanted, looking around the restaurant as if he might spy it on a nearby table.

"Complete," Montanez offered.

"Exactly, Miguel, exactly."

Panama refilled their coffee cups. "Lieutenant Marten, there is a message for you. I will show you the phone."

Balthazar followed her across the room and to the back of the bar. The phone was not off the hook.

She gave a conspiratorial giggle. "I am such a liar. But I saw the expression on your face. I should have told you last night about the mayor's English."

"When I go back, I'll make it plain that my Spanish is adequate."

"Okay, but his Spanish is no better."

"Oh, I see. What is his native language?"

"Spanish," she giggled again. "Couvertier doesn't have full command of any language. But it is all right. He has nothing to say."

As Balthazar returned, the mayor was patting his forehead, careful not to disturb any of the combed strands.

"Please excuse me," Balthazar said in Spanish. "I am sorry for the interruption."

But the little mayor persisted in his choice of language. "I am clearing up the reasons for these bodies. I myself am the doings of these."

"I beg your pardon, sir. You're not saying you're responsible. . . ."

"Yes, yes. Personally. Because I have so many political . . ."

"Rivals," Montanez suggested discreetly.

"Exactly. These men wish to put down my ideas for laying Loiza on the map, for having the *turistas*. . . ."

Panama arrived with plates of fluffy omelets surrounded by thick slices of bright orange papaya. "I make these omelets myself. You will like them. Don't salt them until you try them."

The mayor cut his open eagerly and scooped up a bite of the creamy white center.

"I use the country cheese made here," Panama explained. "And American ham only. The Polish ham has no flavor. And then you see, green pepper, tomato, a bit of onion and green olive. Eat your papaya, too; it's good for your digestion."

"Now," she said as the men fell silent, their mouths full. "Mayor Couvertier has some excellent ideas for promoting Loiza. He thinks because we are such a short distance from San Juan, that as soon as the bridge is completed, we should advertise a great deal more. We have some tourists who come to our Saint's Day fiesta in July. It is held in honor of St. James the Apostle, not our *patronale*, St. Patrick. But, of course, as the mayor will tell you, we had a miracle here. St. James's image appeared. We make the *vejigante* or devil's masks from the coconut. And we make the good people's masks from wire screen. These represent the Knights. Of course, some say the masks of the devils are really to represent the Moors."

She smiled wryly. "Being dark-skinned, of course, they were like devils. "And the mayor thinks that many, many more tourists will eventually come, when the bridge is finished and the road in good repair. So we should build cabins all along the beach. The city has already put up a restaurant and pavilion for dances near *Playa del Mar*."

The mayor nodded happily, his mouth full of egg.

"But," Panama continued, "there are people here who do not agree. They feel that additional buildings would be empty much of the year, as the *Centro Vacacional* is now. The city's beach property is only used in the summer, as well. Let me get you some more toast."

The men ate contentedly, concentrating on the won-

Introducing the first and only complete hardcover collection of Agatha Christie's mysteries

Now you can enjoy the
greatest mysteries ever written
in a magnificent
Home Library Edition.

Discover Agatha Christie's world of mystery, adventure and intrigue

Agatha Christie's timeless tales of mystery and suspense offer something for every reader—mystery fan or not—young and old alike. And now, you can build a complete hardcover library of her world-famous mysteries by subscribing to The Agatha Christie Mystery Collection.

This exciting Collection is your passport to a world where mystery reigns supreme. Volume after volume, you and your family will enjoy mystery reading at its very best.

You'll meet Agatha Christie's world-famous detectives like Hercule Poirot, Jane Marple, and the likeable Tommy and Tuppence Beresford.

In your readings, you'll visit Egypt, Paris, England and other exciting destinations where murder is always on the itinerary. And wherever you travel, you'll become deeply involved in some of the most ingenious and diabolical plots ever invented … "cliff-hangers" that only Dame Agatha could create!

It all adds up to mystery reading that's so good … it's almost criminal. And it's yours every month with The Agatha Christie Mystery Collection.

Solve the greatest mysteries of all time. The Collection contains all of Agatha Christie's classic works including *Murder on the Orient Express, Death on the Nile, And Then There Were None, The ABC Murders* and her ever-popular whodunit, *The Murder of Roger Ackroyd.*

Each handsome hardcover volume is Smythe sewn and printed on high quality acid-free paper so it can withstand even the most murderous treatment. Bound in Sussex-blue simulated leather with gold titling, The Agatha Christie Mystery Collection will make a tasteful addition to your living room, or den.

Ride the Orient Express for 10 days without obligation. To introduce you to the Collection, we're inviting you to examine the classic mystery, *Murder on the Orient Express*, without risk or obligation. If you're not completely satisfied, just return it within 10 days and owe nothing.

However, if you're like the millions of other readers who love Agatha Christie's thrilling tales of mystery and suspense, keep *Murder on the Orient Express* and pay just $9.95 plus postage and handling.

You will then automatically receive future volumes once a month as they are published on a fully returnable, 10-day free-examination basis. No minimum purchase is required, and you may cancel your subscription at any time.

This unique collection is not sold in stores. It's available only through this special offer. So don't miss out, begin your subscription now. Just mail this card today.

☐ Yes! Please send me *Murder on the Orient Express* for a 10-day free-examination and enter my subscription to The Agatha Christie Mystery Collection. If I keep *Murder on the Orient Express*, I will pay just $9.95 plus postage and handling and receive one additional volume each month on a fully returnable 10-day free-examination basis. There is no minimum number of volumes to buy, and I may cancel my subscription at any time.   70110

Name_____

Address_____

City_____ State_____ Zip_____

QB12
Send No Money...
But Act Today!

BUSINESS REPLY MAIL

FIRST CLASS   PERMIT NO. 2154   HICKSVILLE, N.Y.

Postage will be paid by addressee:

The Agatha Christie
Mystery Collection
Bantam Books
P.O. Box 956
Hicksville, N.Y. 11802

derful food. But Balthazar was sighing inwardly; he knew what he would have to ask.

"And these ah . . . rivals, sir. You feel they are putting these bodies on the beach to discredit your administration, to make it seem that you are not doing your job properly?"

"Exactly," the mayor declared, starting in on his papaya. "Now you can see how Terron must be much careful not to arouse these men. People of dignity. Citizens. But you can let them in on the secret. A word only to them. That they are known. Things will then halt."

"Perhaps," Balthazar suggested, "you could give us their names and we could interview them. Discreetly, of course."

"I do not know who these are," the mayor replied, looking meaningfully at Balthazar. "But you will know. A man of craft like you."

Balthazar looked quickly at Sixto, but he was staring straight ahead, chewing thoughtfully.

"Now," Couvertier rose. "Many pardons that I must leave. I am known for my many affairs. Going to necessary meetings. Ah, one idea, you should make the call on the *Norteamericanos.*"

"Yes, sir," Balthazar replied. "Panama gave us the name of the Sterlings."

The little mayor beamed, wiped his mouth and then his hands energetically on his napkin, shook hands all around briskly and went out the door, greeting someone loudly as he exited.

Balthazar took a sip of his coffee and looked at Montanez. "Do you agree with Mayor Couvertier's analysis?"

"It is true that Couvertier plans to run for higher office, unlike myself. Certainly he is very eager to promote this area. You may have noticed all the new unoccupied houses east of town. He thinks that soon people will want to live here, commute to San Juan to work."

He wiped his glasses carefully and stared at them a moment before replacing them. "But I cannot come up with any explanation for those bodies. The local residents are troubled, but I cannot see who could benefit from that. Imagine that someone wanted to lower property values. The property is already very reasonably priced. A fraction of the cost of beachfront land in San Juan. . . . Ah, here's a man who knows real estate—Victor Malen." He beckoned to the man who had just entered.

A heavy-set man in his fifties, wearing an elaborately embroidered linen shirt came over to the table. He listened intently to Montanez's introductions.

"I'm afraid I'm not an expert at all," Malen said slowly, shaking his head and sitting down. He took out a small cigar and rolled it between his fingers. His movements were deliberate, his tall body oddly tense.

"Real estate is only one of my minor interests. I'm semi-retired, but I still own several factories in Haiti. In one they sew baseballs. Used to do it here, but wages got too high. They keep me busy. That," he chuckled, "and my golf game."

Leaning back, he lit his cigar, puffing luxuriously. "Did I ever tell you, Miguel, that my first job in New York was at a country club? I was a busboy. It was a very, very expensive club, but they paid very, very small salaries."

He turned to Balthazar. "I was one of the founding members of our place here. You should talk to some of my friends who live in the condos right on the club's grounds. They're down on the beach. They might be able to shed some light on this . . . nuisance." Taking out an engraved business card, he wrote a few lines on the back. "Give this to the manager. He'll point you in the right direction—and give you a good meal besides. Sorry I can't be of any assistance myself." He went off, trailing cigar smoke.

"Anything else?" Panama came up, her professional smile in place.

"No, thank you," Montanez replied. "But I notice old Albin's donkey tied in back. Not being a bother is he?"

"No, no. He is still on the side of God. I told him

as long as he sticks to knife sharpening and does no more preachings to my customers on the evils of rum, I'll feed him."

"Poor old fellow," the Mayor sighed and explained to the newcomers, "he comes down from the mountains during the winter—says the cold there is too much for his old bones. But he is useful; all the people need their knives and machetes sharpened. The women give him rice and beans for his work. As long as he stays away from liquor, he's no problem. Just wanders around."

He signed the check, and then wiped his glasses again carefully. "Malen's suggestion is a good one. Later in the afternoon, you can catch most of the people at the club. And you should call on the American lady. But don't tell her I suggested it."

"Yes, we will call on the Sterlings," Balthazar said resignedly.

"What? Oh . . . no . . . I meant Emily deDiego."

"American?"

"She came here from Vermont right after her husband's death. It wasn't wise. She and Luis lived here briefly a long time ago, but then left for the United States. She had not been here for many many years, and now she knows no one. When I heard that she wasn't adjusting well, I called and mentioned she might want to sell her land, move back to Vermont. She became very angry—said that Luis told her never to sell. She seemed to think I was trying to buy the land myself, to cheat her in some way. She wouldn't even let me past the gate."

12

"You know what they have in the States that I miss here, Sixto? Population signs."

"Puerto Rico has more than three million people," Sixto said proudly.

"No, I mean individual city signs. When you come to a place, they tell you how many people live in that town. I've never seen any here. And look, Loiza's supposedly a small town. But we drive down this road a mile and a half to the *Centro Vacacional* and people live all along the way. Now we've gone at least a mile further and here's more houses. And I look down the side roads and there's a whole group of houses down each one."

"I can tell you how many people live here," Sixto replied. "Many, many, many. And they and their bicycles and their cars and their children and their dogs and their chickens are all in this road. Their horses are also in this road," he added, referring to the number of small, quick-trotting Puerto Rican horses they had seen with slim young black men riding bareback upon them. "And they did not leave room for parking off this road. And this *Publico* ahead of me is impossible to pass." He leveled an inpatient finger at the modern passenger van ahead of them—one of the public carriers licensed to provide transportation on regular routes at low rates.

Balthazar looked idly out of his window and found himself staring at three large devils' masks made of hollowed-out coconut. They were painted bright blue, with bulging foreheads; three thick teeth stuck out from their gaping mouths. They hung from the porch of a small, rickety building next to the road. Crude coconut candle-holders, toothpick holders and various other small items were advertised for sale.

Finally, Sixto spotted a slight opening in the on-coming traffic and the Chevrolet darted around the van, then slowed abruptly to cross a small bridge. They were immediately in the country again. The tree-lined road turned back slightly toward the sea, lush green fields on either side. More accurately, the coast came up to meet the road. They drove past a wide beach scat-tered with tall palm trees. There was no one on the beach.

The road narrowed again to cross a clear, khaki-colored river. The bridge—only a lane wide—had heavy, waist-high, stone parapets.

Directly across the bridge stood the decaying hulk of a once-beautiful plantation house. Its wide veranda faced the river rather than the road, and it looked as if the overgrown foliage stretched directly to the ocean in back. The high concrete walls facing the road were covered with bright spray-painted graffiti and overhung with equally bright tropical flowers. Above the walls rose the gray and crumbling remains of the third story, thick vines winding in and out of the barren widows.

"This must be where the deDiego woman lives, but it looks deserted," Balthazar said.

They had to drive down the road some distance before finding a wide shoulder on which to park. Walk-ing back, they passed wrought iron gates in the walls, each pitted and flaking, and securely fastened by a heavy rusted chain and padlock that clearly had not been opened for years. Then they saw a narrow open-ing between the parapet of the bridge and the walls, just wide enough to park a car on the short, steep embank-ment of the river.

Going through this, they found the walls ended and a five-foot fence of barbed wire began, with long-needled tropical pines planted closely together just inside. Through the fence they could see a sand driveway with huge stone urns filled with a few straggling plants on either side. Urns stood, two on either side of a wide marble staircase that led to wooden doors that were cracked and splintering. The staircase resumed on the side of the veranda winding up to the second story and then around to the blankness of the third. Only the dusty marble remained impervious to rot.

Arriving at a makeshift gate with a fairly new padlock, they called and called again. Their words echoed in the crumbling house. There was no reply. At last a shabbily dressed man appeared silently. He carried a dark, sturdy candlewood cane, and he wore a wide-brimmed hat and a thickly woven muslin long-sleeved shirt, with ragged trousers. As he approached, they could see he had the narrow face, high cheekbones, and un-lined yellow skin of an Indian. His age was impossible to guess. He reached the gate but made no movement to open it, staring at them as unblinkingly as a lizard.

Sixto pulled out his identification and explained that they wanted to talk to the Señora. Then he asked, "You are the one who found the dead body?"

The man's nod was almost imperceptible. "Then," Sixto added firmly, "we will also need to talk to you." The man glanced over his shoulder at the house and then looked back at them. At last he produced a key and dragged the gate open.

"Could you show us where it was?"

Without speaking, the Indian pointed to the wide strip of white sand at the very edge of the river, just beyond the fence.

"The river is very shallow there? A man could have waded across from the opposite beach?" Balthazar asked.

Again the faint nod.

"If someone came along the beach in back of this house, could you have heard him or seen him?"

The man simply turned and walked away. They followed him down a sandy path that curved between high banyan trees, their fat roots hanging down from their branches. Along the edges of the path were tall, spiky plants topped with yellow-spattered green leaves. Once low-growing border plants, they had not been pruned for years and they had struggled toward the sun. Their thin stalks swayed in the light breeze, and lizards slid up and down the stalks at the men's approach.

The ground sloped gradually to the sea; philoden-dron-like creepers clung to the sandy soil. They passed a square concrete pillar, a broken-off shower head poking through near the top, part of a rusted soap dish still jutting from above the opening for a faucet. Another leaning gate opened onto the beach.

Balthazar looked back at the house. Anyone standing on the first or second story veranda would have seen little of this portion of the beach. It did not look as if anyone would ever again stand on the third story.

The man pointed with his stick to a tiny detached house a considerable distance from both the beach and the larger house. A white horse and a few goats grazed in the field between. "You sleep there?" Sixto asked.

"Manuel, Manuel," a shrill voice called from the plantation house. "Who's there? Who did you let in?"

A frail figure had appeared on the veranda. Balthazar came around the trunk of one of the thick banyans and walked up to the house.

The woman screamed and scrabbled backward. "Not in the daylight! No!" Her protest ended in a ragged sob.

Balthazar called out to her, quietly explaining that they were policemen, as he walked quickly toward her.

She shrank back against the concrete shell of a large outdoor bar as he climbed the staircase. Her gray hair was pulled back into a bun from which a few strands escaped. She was holding her body rigid. She had lost her terrycloth slippers in her terrified motion, and they lay forlornly on one of the few dark red tiles still in place. Her bedraggled, long cotton dress decorated with lingering traces of elegant embroidery, almost covered her dirty bare feet.

Balthazar leaned down and picked up the worn slippers. "I'm sorry I startled you, Mrs. deDiego. My partner and I just wanted to ask a few questions about the dead body on this beach."

The fear in her faded, light-blue eyes did not diminish, but she reached out for the slipper, her hand shaking. "You sound like an American." her voice was accusing. "How did you get here?"

"Actually, I'm on the New York force," Balthazar replied gently, "here on temporary assignment."

She continued to stare at him fearfully. She peered at his thick dark hair, his tanned skin, but stopped at his blue eyes. "Even this close, you look something like Luis when young," she faltered. "Of course, he had brown eyes. He was handsome, too. But you don't sound like him. At night I hear him. Why would they send you here for something like this? Who would have thought they'd bother? Still, they do things so strangely. . . ."

She turned, plucking at her dress, and returned to the house. While Sixto remained behind, trying to coax words from the taciturn caretaker, Balthazar followed her into an enormous room, filled only with spider webs which filigreed the moldings of the vaulted, waterstained ceiling. "I sleep in the small library now. Perhaps that's the mistake? He loved that room."

She turned her anxious face to Balthazar. "I thought to change my room each night, but most of them are unusable. And anyway, he knows this house so well. He grew up here. Besides, I'd hear him whispering in any case. But I explained and explained. He's looking for the other Emily, the young one. Not this old one— not me. She was quite pretty, but I think, looking back on the things I did, a stupid girl, although happy, I remember."

Suddenly she began to dance, twirling slowly around the room as if guided by a partner, murmuring to Balthazar over her shoulder. "We stayed here for a year after we were married. We had dances and many parties on the veranda. We would swim in the ocean when it was hot. The water cistern caught the rain, and then we'd shower outside in the purest rainwater."

She pirouetted with a haunting grace. "Then we moved to Vermont, where I was born. Luis was a professor and we travelled to Europe every summer. We always meant to come back here . . . but Luis and his brother quarreled. He was supposed to be looking after things." Her steps faltered. "We sent him money for repairs and to help pay for the servants. But all the time, there was just Manuel. There was no staff. My brother-in-law lied." She stopped dancing and stared at him pathetically. "He drank up all the money.

"And, you know," she put her hand on Balthazar's arm, squeezing it with surprising strength as if to reassure herself he was solid, "everything man makes falls apart in the tropics. It rusts, or rots, or just comes apart in your hands. And things smell, and they get so dirty, and there are the cockroaches." She began to weep, but not loudly, making no move to wipe away the tears from her furrowed cheeks.

"Perhaps I could make you a cup of tea or coffee, ma'am?" Balthazar asked gently.

She lifted the hem of her dress carefully, showing her thin, veined ankles, and wiped her eyes. "Yes, yes, I often have coffee at this time of the morning. I get some peace walking on the beach. Then I have coffee. Come into the kitchen."

It was a long room, furnished with an old table, battered cabinets, a teetering metal stool, and two unmatched chairs. At the other end was a small stove. She gestured toward a dented enamel coffee pot. Balthazar put it on the one burner that worked, found two chipped cups.

She arranged her dress primly, as she sat down. "I still use rainwater for the coffee. It's much better." Balthazar eyed the huge, above-ground cistern beyond the kitchen window dubiously. It looked like an abandoned railroad tanker car set on high, concrete stilts, and its corroded surface was thick with ancient rust.

A little color seeped back to her face as she drank the strong coffee, but her eyes still roamed the room. "Things move around here so quickly," she said nervously. "Running things. I see them out of the corner of my eyes. Manuel says not to kill the spiders and lizards because then things would be worse. How could it be worse? The air you breathe is full of gnats. They go up your nose and stick in the back of your throat. Have you noticed?"

"Have you lived here long, Mrs. deDiego?" Balthazar asked.

"Since Luis died. I'm not sure when that was—some months," she replied vaguely. "I brought him back here to be buried. He was sick a long time. It took all the money."

"You own this land, though?"

"Luis said not to sell," she said fiercely. "He said it was valuable."

"Is it? Has anyone tried to buy it?"

"When I first came back. I had just seen the house and I was crying and crying. A black man came. I didn't talk to him. I never talk to blacks. I don't like them. They'll only cheat you. Manuel said there was a body of one on the beach—not to go out that day. Then some blacks came, pretending to be policemen."

"Do you know how the body got there?"

"Yes," she said unhesitatingly, "the sea brought it. The sea spits everything up on the beach that it doesn't want. I see it all in the morning—rotting fish, seaweed, pieces of old wood, coconuts with long hair that look just like heads, rolling back and forth, back and forth in the waves." She squeezed her pale blue eyes shut.

"Have you ever thought of going back to Vermont? Do you have family or friends there?"

"Everyone I knew is dead—or gone. They moved away because it was so cold there. But I can't move in any case, you see. I have no money. I would have to sell the land. What would Luis say? I promised. And I don't want to tell him, but I don't really think the land is worth anything."

*   *   *

"If someone is trying to frighten that poor lady," Balthazar said, getting back into the car, "they're going about it the wrong way. I have the feeling she'd just step right over a corpse and continue her morning stroll."

"Sí," Sixto said, "and *Navieras de Puerto Rico* could unload the cargo for the entire island on the beach, and the caretaker wouldn't mention it."

"She makes some sense, though," Balthazar said, looking around. "I don't think her land is especially valuable—there's a lot of vacant land here. We can do a little fishing expedition later at the country club, see what the members have to say about real estate in the area. It's very close, but I'm sure the mayor is right: everyone is out golfing or playing tennis right now. Might as well see what Terron's got now and hit them later in the afternoon."

13

". . . WHEN THEY SEE these two women together on the putting green, and the first golfer says, 'My God, there's my wife and my mistress!' And the second golfer . . ." Fred McMurdie was laughing so hard that he could barely bring out the punch line, ". . . he says, 'That's just what I was going to say.' " He roared and pounded the table, fighting for breath. The three tall glasses of Scotch and water jiggled precariously. Balthazar's face hurt: he felt he had used a lifetime's supply of polite smiles. Sixto was staring with glazed eyes at the sunset-colored ocean through the high glass wall of the country club.

Showing them the tennis court, McMurdie had told tennis jokes; introducing them to the funeral director, he had told corpse jokes; spotting a retired South American general, he had found inspiration for military jokes. They had just finished a brief tour in one of the many shiny golf carts lined up beside the green (he had known only three golf-cart jokes); they were now seated comfortably in the bar. He was now on golf jokes.

When Balthazar had tried desperately to get back to the subject of the interview—the corpses of the black men on the beach—McMurdie had launched into Rastus-and-'Liza jokes. He dismissed the problem with a wave of his hand. Blacks and Hispanics always had rival gangs. They were just trying to frighten each other, he assured them.

Since McMurdie had insisted on ordering a lavish

dinner for the three of them, Balthazar looked bleakly ahead at the evening. If McMurdie, by some ill chance, found that Balthazar was half-Irish, they would hear all the Pat-and-Mike jokes. Worse, McMurdie had started his career as a traveling salesman.

He looked like a man who had spent life genially picking up the bar tab for his customers. His red hair was turning gray and his large nose was turning red. Patting his firm round belly and letting his belt out a notch, he said that his doctor had ordered him to give up food, wine, women, and song. So, he chortled, he'd switched to Scotch and given up singing. McMurdie's delight in finding an English-speaking audience for his humor knew no limits. Throughout the afternoon, he had repeatedly expressed his pleasure that Vic Malen had sent them over.

Malen's card had, Balthazar thought at first, proved useful. The manager of the country club, a nervous young Puerto Rican, had been hesitant about disturbing the members. Going over his records, he had established that only one person currently at the club's condos had been in residence during the relevant times. That person was Malen's business associate, Mr. McMurdie. Balthazar had produced the card. With obvious relief, the manager had called Mr. McMurdie.

"How long have you been in business with Mr. Malen?" Balthazar asked while McMurdie was still catching his breath.

"Oh, Vic and me—we go back a long time. See, I was traveling for one of the big sports-equipment nationals ten, twelve years ago. He was headwaiter then at La Paloma. A lot of my customers moved up, became vice presidents of companies, but they'd started in sports themselves. And they liked Mex food. La Paloma in New York, you know, is the best—the most expensive. So I started cutting a deal with Vic—he was Señor Victor then, everybody knew him. He added to the tab, then gave me—"

He stopped, obviously remembering they were policemen. "Oh, just tax stuff—write-offs. Anyway, I told him the real money was in making the sports stuff. It's labor-intensive, see—uniforms, baseballs, all the crap that's gotta be sewed. Labor was cheap then in Puerto Rico. And the U.S. Government was pushing the island—great tax write-offs. Gotta leave a certain amount of capital here, but then no tax on it. And Vic—he's sharp, thinks like an accountant. You got to do that these days. He speaks Spanish, knew the territory here; I know it in New York. So we got together. Now, our factories are in Haiti and the Dominican Republic. Lot cheaper. You gotta pay minimum wage here."

"You must travel back and forth to Hispaniola quite often then?"

"Oh, yeah, and New York, South America. But this is my home base. Or as near as I get to one. Great place. Look at this." He waved his arm expansively around the club. "Just like home."

Balthazar, on first seeing the country club, had thought that, given its appearance, it could well have been located outside any upper–middle-class suburb in the Sun Belt. The clubhouse, the condos, the pro shack, with their peach-colored brick and terra cotta roofs, were all vaguely Spanish in architecture. Members had all the amenities: a large, paved parking lot, a close-trimmed emerald course, and tennis courts.

"And," McMurdie continued, gesturing for another Scotch, "the U.S. ain't ever gonna let go of Puerto Rico. We got these big bases here and you need something you can count on in the Caribbean. Hell, the Puerto Ricans know they got a deal, too. They've been American citizens since 1917. So they can go to the States, get a legal job. Not like the Mexicans. Plus here they get food stamps, welfare checks, Social Security. Right?" He clapped Sixto heartily on the shoulder.

"Let me tell you, you don't know where you are even one island over. Back in the fifties when Havana was roaring, everybody having a good time, making a nice piece of change, who'd have thought they'd go Commie? Now, you look at the Dominican Republic. Who knows? And Haiti—that's one weird place. All those poor niggers, begging, hanging on your arm when you walk down the street. They call you Papa." He winked and nudged Balthazar. "Maybe a few, but I ain't got *that* many black bastards over there!"

"You think your investments are safe there?"

"Who knows? Me and Vic—we weren't sure at first. It was okay when Papa Doc was running it. One smart fellow. But could his kid run the place? Not for long, it turns out. I got a lady friend there. Speaks French and the other singsongy stuff, too. She's real light-skinned. Sharp. Big help. She tells me that old Duvalier studied Voodoo before he took over. He even ran this Bureau of Ethnology or whatever. Probably found Voodoo useful, you know." He tapped Balthazar's arm. "You be careful if you go over there. I mean about the ladies. Disease. AIDS. Who knows?"

"You still have investments in Puerto Rico, sir?"

"Call me Fred. 'Sir' is too much like the goddamned Army. Say, did I tell you the one about the Sergeant who—"

"Yes," said Balthazar decisively. "About your investments. . . ."

"I just thought of something. Didn't you say your first name was Balthazar? Don't tell me they call you . . . ?" Even his stomach shook with laughter.

"Zar. My friends call me Zar," Balthazar interjected hurriedly—but too late.

"Balls." McMurdie was strangling with laughter. "Did I tell you the one about the guy who found first one golf ball, then a little further on another golf ball, and pretty soon he came across a dead golf?"

The waiter brought their salads. Avocado halves had been scooped out and filled with pineapple, oranges, avocado and bright red cherries.

"Try it," McMurdie urged, stabbing an avocado with his fork. "They put on olive oil, vinegar and some lime juice. Sounds funny, but I got so I kinda like this fruit stuff. But for the main course—don't worry. I know what you boys need—good, thick, juicy steak.

Raise a lot of cattle here in P.R. Wouldn't have thought it."

"You were telling us about your investments in Puerto Rico," Balthazar prodded.

"Oh, yes. Our company—Malmac—is based here. And see what we did. Did you know that if you're a citizen of Puerto Rico, they don't tax your rental income? Sweet deal. So when we moved out, we rented our factories to the electronics companies. They wanted to take a look-see here—got a pretty well-educated group of workers on the island. So what they've got to pay them minimum—it's still a hell of a lot less than they'd pay people in the States. And they don't want to put their expensive equipment on some island that might go Commie. No big problem for us—bunch of sewing machines."

"Given this favorable tax situation, do you own a lot of real estate here?" Balthazar asked.

"You have to be a citizen of Puerto Rico to get that tax break. Well, it's not much different than being a U.S. citizen—you just pay P.R. taxes instead of U.S. and you can't vote in national elections unless you're in the States—but still. . . . There's other ways around taxes. Mind you, even when your write-offs are perfectly legal, you can't get most accountants to cut them too fine. No way. They're afraid of an audit. See, they got to sit and hold your hand for nothing if you're audited. And if the IRS doesn't like what some accountant does, they can audit all his accounts. Bankruptcy city. The accountants put you third on the list—after themselves and Uncle Sam."

The steaks the waiter put in front of them were thick, rare, and lightly covered with ox-tail sauce. They were delicious. "In Puerto Rico you always order french fries," McMurdie said. "They make them fresh. Can't get over that. But I got the potato salad, too. They make it just the way my mother did. 'Course I told them here at the club to leave out the green peas. My mother—God rest her sainted soul—never put in green peas. Say," he looked at Balthazar with a gleam in his eye, "was your mother Irish?"

"She died when I was very young," Balthazar said hastily. "I was raised by my aunt—she was Dutch. My last name was originally spelled with two *a*'s."

"Dutch, huh? Yeah, like St. Maarten's here in the Caribbean. There were these two guys standing by a hole in the dike and—"

"What you're saying about investments is very interesting," Balthazar interrupted, with a glance at Sixto, whose face was stony.

"You gotta think about these things. You got any investments?" McMurdie asked Balthazar shrewdly.

"My aunt invested my parent's insurance pretty well in stocks and bonds."

"No good. Uncle Sam takes too big a bite out of whatever you make. Here's what you do. Buy rental property. Good deal even under our tax system. But, you gotta get a partner in uniform. He collects the rents in his cop suit. People pay on the dime. Collecting rent's a hell of a problem. Vic says that's why he doesn't mess with rentals. He's got a lot of different companies anyway. Hell, I think everybody does. Politicians and all. Perfectly legal, though, perfectly legal."

The waiter appeared with three large slices of golden, meringue-topped coconut pie.

"They take good care of you here," McMurdie said with satisfaction. "Almost like home. Few things take some getting used to, of course. Sometimes I think everybody here with any get-up-and-go got up and went to New York."

He laughed and thumped Sixto on the back. "No offense. And they still hang on to some pretty queer ideas, especially out here. Vic was just telling me that some of the old folks his Mom knew were after him to get one of the Voodoo witch doctors from Haiti over here. Made him laugh till he nearly wet his pants after they left. But he's a good guy. Said why not pick up the check? Give 'em a little party. Have some fun. Waiter, another round of Scotch for the troops here."

The waiter took away the empty glasses and Sixto's untouched one and brought three more.

"What was I sayin'? Oh yeah, funny ideas. Wait'll I tell you what happened to me yesterday. We got this young black girl that cleans our units. Great ass, smiles nice, but I can't talk to her much because she's got no English. Anyway, the other day she was making up the bed when I came in and I thought, what the hell, you don't have to speak the language to get your point across. So I grab her tit and just give her a friendly little squeeze. She backs up some but she doesn't say anything. So I really gave it a feel. Out falls this little pillow with a charm on it. I picked it up. She got all excited. Never saw anything like it in my life. She started screaming and ran right at me. Hysterical. I thought she was going to kill me. All over some damn little good-luck charm." He shook his head. "These people got funny ideas."

The night was still and warm as they left the country club and strolled toward the brightly-lighted parking area. Balthazar's head throbbed painfully. "I've an idea, Sixto," he said as Sixto unlocked the car door. "But it may be the effects of those drinks. Good thing you're driving."

Sixto sighed. "Scotch always tastes like something I have to drink because it's good for me."

"I was wondering if you could smuggle drugs into the States in baseballs."

"Baseballs?"

"Just the other day, some South Americans were caught smuggling cocaine powder inside of geodes of lapis lazuli. Those rocks are the same size as baseballs. McMurdie's been in that business for some time. Customs would have no cause to suspect him."

"Why would such a rich man smuggle drugs?" Sixto pulled out onto the now-deserted road.

"To get richer. The more money you have, the

plainer it is that you've won the game. That would please McMurdie."

They approached the dark fields of the deDiego land; the moon glinted on the blacktop road. "Of course, I haven't worked out how—" Balthazar began, and then leaned forward, "Look out!"

Directly ahead, a large school bus without lights roared at high speed across the narrow bridge, heading straight for them. In front of them was the concrete parapet of the bridge, to the side the high, solid walls of the deDiego estate. Sixto wrenched the wheel, hit the accelerator, and dove for the small space that led to the river. The wide Chevrolet cleared it exactly, and spun down the short embankment, landing with a metallic thud in the soft sand of the river bottom. Even at that steep angle, the shallow water just covered the top of the hood.

Balthazar had thrown his hands against the dashboard. The force of their fall jolted his wrists painfully. He winced as he flexed them, then he sucked in his breath and saw Sixto slumped forward, his head against the steering wheel. He grabbed his arm. "Are you all right?"

Without lifting his head, Sixto replied weakly, "Sí."

They sat in silence for a long moment.

"My God, if we'd hit that wall or that bridge, we'd have been smashed. I can't believe what you did—that was the best move I ever saw. But that guy, he was trying to get us. He was, wasn't he?"

"Jesu . . Jesu . . . "

"Are you trying to say you saw who it was? Was it the mayor? Jesus Couvertier?"

"No," Sixto said, finally raising his head and staring at Balthazar bleakly. "I'm praying."

"God," Balthazar said, "just think, Sixto. If we hadn't been here today, if you hadn't noticed this . . . I mean . . . somebody must have been praying. What luck."

Sixto reached over and pulled the keys from the ignition. From his key chain dangled the first four beads of a rosary. In place of a cross there was a small shining silver sword. He held it up. "My mama gave this to me when I joined the *Policia*. The sword of justice. Of course we are safe."

Balthazar picked up the radio receiver and clicked the button. There was no response. He tried again, and then again.

Sixto leaned over with a small groan, unbuckled his holster and gun from his ankle, slipped off his shoes, and rolled up his pants.

Balthazar did the same. "Some fishing trip," he groused.

He looked at the half-submerged car and the surrounding sand, shimmering peacefully in the moonlight. He thought of the stone wall they had so nearly missed. He laughed, a little too loudly, as relief washed over him. Beside him, Sixto began to laugh, too.

They waded across the river and up the other embankment, carrying their shoes, still laughing.

14

IT WAS NOT YET DAWN. Balthazar tried to remember where he was. He stretched and found that his whole body—not only his still mending knee—was stiff. The accident, he thought—probably the after-effect of the adrenalin sizzling through his veins.

Almost always he awoke slowly, the memories of the previous day coming back one at a time. But some came back slightly changed from their night's journey through the subconscious. It took awhile to recognize them in their new configurations. As if the mind, he mused, sorted like a computer while one slept, regrouping, rearranging the day's activities.

The image of the school bus hurtling toward them came to his mind in the unfamiliar darkness like a black-and-white photograph. He looked at it carefully. The driver high up and invisible. It was ominous and odd. School buses always moved slowly, bulkily, plodding at a maddening pace ahead of you on a narrow road. The familiar school bus, the civilized representation of a community, coming down like a rattling juggernaut. . . .

One of the night's dreams came back to him. He was a child again, standing alone in the center of a ring of other children holding hands in a schoolyard. It was twilight, and he couldn't see very well. He knew the game, but he couldn't remember its name and that was important. He didn't know what he was supposed to do next, either. All of the other children were black, their faces expressionless. The circle grew tighter and tighter, as if they were driven by their own fear of the outer darkness behind them. But they feared him, too, and wished to hold him in. He pitied them, but he was angry.

The dream made him think of something Maira had said on the phone the previous evening. He had not told her of the accident. It was, he had to admit, partly because of his need to protect her, to keep her from worry—a feeling he knew she did not like. He said he'd called to say he missed her. But she had sensed something in his voice. Too much emotion perhaps: he had only been gone two days; she was only twenty miles away. So he told her about Loiza Aldea, the impression he had of people and things slipping away from him, scuttling off like the crabs, looking hostile.

Their relationship was still at the stage when two people faced each other in wonder. Soon they would have to move, to contemplate standing nearer or even side by side. Then the prickly questions would arise. Surely he would have to return to New York soon. Yet her work was here, her fragile sense of home was here, as well as that of her five-year-old nephew, Rico, who lived with her.

But now everything that was said delighted the hearer. She was fascinated by all his stories about the town, about the terror the mutilated bodies apparently thrown up by the sea was causing. She asked about the people involved in the case.

"An American couple named Sterling?" she had asked. "Felicity Sterling? Imagine. I read all her books to Rico. His favorite one is *The Sky Farmer*—I have to read it once a week. I bet I have it memorized. She writes the best children's books. And her husband, Josh Sterling. You don't recognize the name? He's a jewelry designer; every month his work is featured on one of the inside front pages of *The New Yorker*. Sterling by Sterling. Or Sterling Gold. He illustrates her books. Witty, abstract drawings. Something for children to use their imaginations on." She'd heard that they lived some-where in Puerto Rico part of the year.

That was the connection with the dream, of course. Children's books. Children's games. He got up quietly and put on his swimming suit.

In the other room, Sixto was sleeping, curled in the middle of the bed. The sheet was wrapped around him, covering even his shoulders. February was winter to Sixto. Balthazar decided not to wake him—he scribbled a short note and went out silently.

Now it was getting much lighter, but the sky was still gray. He decided he might just sit on the beach until the sun rose. But when he was actually standing on the sands, the waves looked tempting. He braced himself and plunged in.

Ten minutes later, he was floating lazily on his back just past the breakers. The choppy ocean felt more like the rinse cycle of a washer than a whirlpool bath but the soreness in his muscles was gone. He looked up and saw a large coconut bobbing purposefully toward him a short distance down the beach. A white coconut. No, it was a swimmer, a bald man swimming steadily and without effort towards him.

The swimmer stopped about five feet from Balthazar, standing up to his massive chest in the water. He was in his late forties. His eyes were very blue, his eyebrows and moustache very blond. He looked like one of Kaiser Wilhelm's generals who had put aside his spiked helmet for a swim, an impression that was softened by his wide boyish smile.

"Great time for swimming, isn't it," he boomed.

"Once you get in," Balthazar responded with a grin.

"Knew you were an American, even from way down the beach."

"How?"

"Easy. You're swimming at this time of the morn-ing, at this time of the year, although you're the first one I've seen in our waters, so to speak. Felicity and I feel as if we own this beach because we're about the only ones who use it most of the winter. Except for the joggers on the beach, of course."

"You're Josh Sterling?"

"Right. Recognized the bald head, I bet. I shave it every morning. People always remember it. You must be the detective from New York. Sorry about your accident."

Balthazar stared.

Sterling laughed heartily. "Shouldn't tell you how I know . . . But Terron came by last night. He really wanted to talk to Jorge, who lives in back of us on our property. Works for us part-time. But he's a mechanic and does quite a bit of work for the city. So he has a key to the community lot—where they keep the school buses and garbage trucks. Terron asked about Jorge's key, and he also mentioned you might be coming by."

"Yes, the Sergeant thought that, given the location of your house, you might be of some help."

"Come any time after twelve. We work in the morning." Sterling waved in a friendly manner and dove back under the water.

Terron frowned down at the papers on the table in front of him. "Could have been one of our school buses, of course. We keep them in the fenced area next to the cemetery. Five keys to the padlock around that we know of, one on a big board in the mayor's office. Labeled. But if someone borrowed one of ours, he'd risk being seen coming and going. Not much of a risk, given the location of the lot, but some. No way to know yet and the problem is that all the buses had to be driven this morning. Checked them all for anything obvious, but we were working in the dark, mostly. Buses have to be on the road pretty early."

They were sitting in a small dusty room off the main area of the police station. The pile of reports in front of Terron was surprisingly thick. "What we're looking at now is how many buses there are that aren't school buses. When the mileage gets up, they sell them to churches, local groups, one even to a rock group that plays at the small bars in the area. Some of these are repainted, but not all." He scowled at Balthazar and Sixto. "Pretty sure it was yellow?" They nodded.

"But," he went on, "I'm not so sure that it was deliberate. Some young kid taking the bus back after he's dropped off the rest of the group. He sees the empty road and decides it'd be fun to see what the old bus can do. Probably shocked the hell out of him, seeing you come around the corner."

Balthazar said nothing. He and Sixto had discussed that possibility but, remembering the incident, neither could even visualize a shape behind the wheel, much less the terrified face of a teenager. Instinct said a deliberate attempt had been made to drive them off the road. Both had shared the eerie feeling that the bus had not even had a driver.

"Speaking of young men, what do you think of the idea that the body dumping has something to do with youth gangs playing macho tricks or even giving some kind of territorial warning to each other?" Balthazar asked.

Terron scratched his chin. "Nobody here at the station thought it likely. One thing, we think we'd have heard something about that. Closest thing we got to an organized gang is the car club. Damndest thing. About twelve of these young guys got late model Toyota Corollas. They put these little tires on them and once a week they all get together at the service station down the road and line them up. Play the radios, wipe off their cars. Try to out-polish each other. When they're waiting for the light to change up on Highway 3, they jump out of their cars and pull rags out of plastic bags. Wipe the car down every time they stop."

He walked to the soft drink machine, kicked it, took out three cans, and handed them around. "Not to say there isn't the usual stuff. I looked back at the incident reports a while back. One of the local kids got into it with a Hogar Crea guy. They were fighting in back of the baseball stadium. Over a girl. And your drunk fights. Lot of those. Breaking and entering. Common, but not gangs doing it. Just too many young men, too few jobs. Bound to get into trouble."

Terron's voice became brisker now that he could recommend action. "We got a car you can use. I made a list of some of the older people on the beach that you could talk to. Drew some directions by their names. Given the roads where you're going, a jeep would be good. But all ours are the blue and white ones with police markings. They'll see you coming and hide out. Of course, they'll know you're police as soon as they get a look at you. But they won't know until then. Not," he chuckled mysteriously, "by looking at this car, anyway. It's one your Narcotics boys confiscated in San Juan and sent down here. Decided it might not be the thing for detectives there. Hasn't got a police radio, but it's got everything else."

He handed them a list and some sketchily drawn maps. "Don't know if you'll get anything. People didn't want to talk to me, but it's worth a try. Oh, had your car towed over to San Isidro. Mechanic says it'll take a couple days. He thought it was funny, said 'your Chevrolet *No va.*' " Terron guffawed.

"Certainly doesn't," Balthazar said drily.

Terron looked thoughtful. "Could probably get you a couple horses from the Mounted Police in the *Piñones*."

Balthazar stood up hastily. He wasn't sure if Terron was joking, but he vividly remembered the last time he was on horseback—a pony ride when he was four.

"No, *gracias*," Balthazar and Sixto spoke in unison.

15

THE STERLING'S HOUSE stood on a corner, alone at the end of a long road. One side faced the road, the other the beach. Next to it was a big empty lot, a faded For Sale sign slanting sideways. Across the road, chickens scratched industriously in the big field of palms and pines.

A four-foot stone wall, topped with eight feet of chain link fence and then barbed wire, surrounded the house. Inside the fence were rows of tall, thick tropical pines. There was a wide yard, covered only with pine needles. Flowering shrubs concealed most of the lower half of the large white house. The upper half was covered with shiny black wrought iron. Heavy screens in back of the grillwork blocked all view of the inside. The house seemed to pull back inside of itself, holding outsiders at arm's length. There was no doorbell on the gate.

But as Balthazar and Sixto parked, the gate swung open. At the top of the inner driveway, the wrought iron door pulled back and an inner door rolled up slowly. Josh Sterling stood in the doorway, barefoot, dressed in a crisp white shirt and white cotton shorts, smiling. He looked even taller than he had appeared that morning. Balthazar introduced Sixto and, looking back at the gate sliding shut, asked curiously, "How do people get in touch with you?"

"They can't," Josh answered. "But I have my workshop right here on the veranda so I can see who's outside the gate. We have a good security system. Have to."

The veranda was long and as wide as a room. It was lined on one side with work benches; most were covered with clear plastic dropcloths. Beneath the plastic, there were tools of all kinds: pliers, hammers, screwdrivers, vises, clamps, as well as an expensive-looking collection of electric equipment. On shelves above the work benches were boxes with small plastic drawers and still more tools in plastic bags.

Scattered around the workbenches and hanging on the walls were snorkeling equipment, scuba equipment, fishing equipment. In one corner an inflated rubber boat held more: spear guns, lobster hooks, fishing nets. Across the veranda stood a large drafting table, cluttered with fat artist's pencils, thin paintbrushes, colored markers, half-finished sketches.

"Have to keep the jewelry tools covered—sea air gets to 'em," Sterling told them, gesturing towards the workbenches. He pointed to the plastic boxes on the shelves. "Up there I've got my stone collection. I set them myself in my necklaces and bracelets. I just keep the semi-precious ones here, all sorted by size. Amethysts, quartz, malachite, amber, coral, tourmaline, garnets. You wouldn't believe the colors of those stones: purples, blues, deep reds, pinks, clear yellows. Beautiful when they're cut properly. You can get most of them pretty cheap here in the Caribbean. But I don't keep the gold here. Too much of a temptation for burglars."

He pointed to the littered drafting table, chuckling. "I try to keep my jewelry design drawings separate from the illustrations of 'Liss's books, but you can see, they don't stay separate." There was an exquisitely detailed drawing of a small boy peering at what looked like a tropical forest, flowers drooping down and vines climbing up. In one corner, a bracelet with a square faceted stone had been sketched in.

"It looks disorganized, but I know where everything is," Sterling said. "Come on in. Felicity is probably ready to stop work."

They turned the corner of the veranda, and there were couches and chairs of white rattan with cushions of pure blues and purples and whites. Stretching out ahead, as if part of the decor, was the blue of the ocean. Between the wide expanses of screen and grillwork hung flowering plants, and there were more plants in every corner and on most of the glass-topped tables.

"I don't know how she does it, but everywhere we go, my wife finds a maid who always wanted to be a gardener. Luckily, Rosie's husband here is a mechanic who doesn't mind yardwork outside. Not that there's much here. Only certain plants like the sea air and they look after themselves." He gestured toward the long backyard filled with hibiscus, cactus, and palm, then pointed to a small house at the end of the yard. "Rose and Jorge live in back. It's a good arrangement. Always someone to watch the house. Burglar alarms aren't much use. It takes the police too long to get here. You saw what our road's like. And we spend the summers back in the States."

When Felicity Sterling came in, carrying a plastic ice bucket, Balthazar sucked in his breath in surprise. Somehow he had imagined a plump, white-haired, grandmotherly author of children's books. Although Felicity's skin was Caribbean coffee-colored, her black ancestry was evident. Her long neck, her beautifully shaped head with its closely-cropped black hair, her thick-lidded, almond-shaped eyes resembled the museum statues from Equatorial Africa. She wore a printed cotton caftan in soft earth tones.

"How nice to meet you," she said. "I've read all about you both." Her low contralto voice was warm, with the faintest of British intonations. "We always have white wine and fruit at this time. It makes us think we're having lunch. Or there's beer, of course."

"I'll get the drinks," Josh said firmly. "You sit down."

Directing the two detectives to the couch opposite her with a wave of amazingly long and perfectly manicured fingers, she seated herself, gracefully erect. "The case you're working on fascinates us," she told them, "given our background. Josh and I were both born in Jamaica—British mothers and American fathers. But, of course, neither of us can quite work out what the motive would be. The bodies might frighten people away, but they also call attention to the beach. And no one goes out at night, anyway. Josh and I hardly ever miss the full moon rising each month—it's an amazing sight. But we never see anyone else out, even then. Still, Josh is leaning toward smugglers using fear to keep people away."

"What's *your* favorite theory?" Balthazar asked. He felt himself pulled into her spell, but didn't resist it. Beside him, Sixto sat silent, obviously enchanted.

"It has to have something to do with Voodoo, to use the more familiar Haitian word for the traditional African beliefs of the Caribbean blacks. We call it *obeah* in Jamaica. The Puerto Ricans use the term *santeria*. There are differences, just as there are differences in doctrine in the various Christian sects. But people really misunderstand Voodoo. True, small animals are sacrificed, and then eaten. This rite is done in the same spirit as the symbolic Christian one where red wine is substituted for the blood of the sacrificial lamb, the scapegoat, and bread for the body. But an ignorant white man years ago wrote a lurid book about the practices of the Haitians, making them sound like a group of bloodthirsty black savages." She gestured with angry impatience.

Josh returned, carrying a tray with a bottle of white wine, bottles of imported beer with beads of moisture, and chilled glasses. "That's not a cushion by 'Liss's feet. It's a soapbox," he said with an affectionate, but worried, smile. "In graduate school, her dissertation was on Voodoo."

"I'll hurry up and finish the lecture by the time you've sliced the fruit."

"Sure," he said. "I believe that," and turned back to the kitchen.

"The misuse of Voodoo's power does make me

angry," she said earnestly. "The beliefs of Voodoo reassure its followers. The poor feel they have no control over their lives, feel there's no way for them to escape bad luck. They never even hope for good luck. But Voodoo tells them that they are surrounded by spirits—in the water, the trees, everywhere—that care about their problems—spirits that are very like themselves. They need to pay attention to these *loa*, honor them, even feed them, but the spirits can protect them."

She grimaced. "Yet there are places in the Caribbean—although I wouldn't have thought in Puerto Rico—that these very beliefs are used to frighten the people even more. Those in power use the ideas for their own ends, particularly the powerful fear of *zombis*."

"It's not clear to me why that idea is so terrifying."

"One rubs this powerful poison into a living person's flesh and he is paralyzed. His breath and heart rate slow to almost nothing. But he remains conscious. In at least one case, the man was pronounced dead by a Western doctor and then buried—alive. All semblance of life is gone, and the person has no control over what happens to him. But he knows he has no control. Isn't it like the worst fears we have of an afterlife, too? Something terrible is happening to you, and you *realize* it." She shuddered.

"But can they really do that?"

"Yes. The poison of the puffer fish is used. It's so deadly that in Japan, where the fish is a delicacy, only a few specialized chefs can prepare it."

"They eat a poison fish?" Sixto looked disconcerted.

"Eating the flesh gives you a euphoric feeling. If the right amount is used in turning someone into a *zombi*, then it wears off. The "body" is dug up again, and other drugs of the tranquilizer family are administered to maintain control of the person. Modern psychiatric medicine really progressed when scientists turned to the knowledge of plants that South American and African tribesmen had. The slaves brought to the Caribbean in the eighteenth century came largely from Benin and Nigeria. I had a Nigerian graduate student, a very sophisticated man, who told me amazing stories about practices today in his homeland. Of course, Voodoo here is a conglomeration of ideas. The slaves added what they learned from the colonists, their masters, to their body of beliefs."

She looked out at the ocean, sadly. "You can imagine how those slaves felt. Packed in the holds of those awful ships and then treated abominably when they arrived. No doubt they thought they were *zombis*. One of the beliefs they had was that if you gave *zombis* salt, they would realize they were dead and hurry back to the grave. Perhaps it was an explanation for the wretched food they were given. But Voodoo offered them other, happier explanations, too. It kept them from despair, and gave them hope. Authentic Voodoo ceremonies are joyous occasions."

"Your feeling is that these bodies are meant as a reminder of what can happen to people, a reminder from their pasts?" Balthazar asked slowly. "But these bodies were already dead before being shot in the temple. They were even embalmed. The people here would know that, surely."

"It depends, doesn't it, on what you mean by saying people "know" anything. Do they trust what they're told? Most of the people here usually just finish high school, and most of the older ones never got that far. And they've been told Voodoo stories since they were small. What we learn as children becomes so much a part of us that it is never re-examined when we grow up. It's very difficult, even for the highly educated, to take those ideas and beliefs out of their heads and look at them objectively."

She gestured eloquently. "So many people go through life like wind-up dolls, repeating actions that are clearly unwise, spouting ideas that have no relevance. They might as well be *zombis*. That's how I became interested in writing children's books. I believe you can tell children a great deal more than you can tell adults."

Josh Sterling had returned with the fruit and had

been eying his wife uneasily during the discussion. But his face cleared at the subject change. "Liss's books are wonderful. Selling well, too."

"*Our* books, Josh. Your drawings are what makes them sell."

"Have you an idea of what people are being warned against?" Balthazar asked.

Josh shook his head. "Not really. The person in back of it—what can he gain? What does he want people to do? And which people?"

Felicity smiled. "I should tell you that although Josh is an artist, he had a long training as a business-man. So he always looks for the profit motive. I have to agree it's a starting place. But it's *our* starting place. You have to realize that things are different here in Loiza, despite the fact that American products are sold every-where. It's been a fairly closed community for some time."

"You've been coming here for a few years?"

"We've been spending winters here for four years now," Felicity replied, with an affectionate glance at her husband. "We drove all around the island when we first came. We wanted a place that was out of the way, but near the conveniences of a large modern city. There are so many beautiful places on both the west and east coasts of Puerto Rico, but most were too far from San Juan. And we have the world's best beach here. Perfect waves, not just a smooth and glassy sea. Very few people use it in the winter, although I understand it's quite crowded in the summer."

"Your wife said you liked the smuggling theory, Mr. Sterling?"

"It's a perfect beach for smuggling," he chuckled. "And the location of the reefs makes it unlikely any-where else."

"Where are the reefs here?"

"Oh, I can show you," Sterling rose enthusiasti-cally. "Before we came down the first time, I got all the charts and maps from the U.S. Geological Survey Of-fice. I wanted to find a good body-surfing beach, and, of course, reefs block the large waves. 'Liss, where are those charts?"

"Probably with all those rolled-up blueprints and maps by your third workbench," she answered serenely, picking up an apple.

"Yes," he beckoned to the two men. Rounding the corner again, he rummaged in a plastic wastebasket stuffed with tall rolls of paper standing upright. He pulled out one thick roll and spread it out on his workbench.

"Here's the Loiza river. For three-quarters of a mile west to San Juan through the *Piñones*, there are no reefs. Now for three-quarters of a mile down this way, past the center where you're staying just to our house here, there aren't any either. And the water is six fathoms—thirty-six feet—deep. You could get a nice-sized boat in—one with a two or three foot draft. Say a twenty-five to thirty foot boat. That's the best spot— and it's close to San Juan. You'd want to avoid most of the rest of the east coast. Too busy around Fajardo. Lots of other boats and then there's the big naval base at Roosevelt Roads."

Moving his finger around the charted island, he added, "Pretty shallow around Ponce, but there are some fishing villages near it. I'd guess you'd run into high waves around Rincón. If I were coming from South America—and we're less than five hundred miles from there—I'd sure put Loiza high on the list."

There were five or six different maps beneath the chart. They slipped out beneath the top one. Sterling rolled them up hastily as his wife entered.

"So often when guests come," she said, turning to smile at Balthazar and Sixto, "they disappear into Josh's workshop, and hours later he's still showing off his stones or demonstrating his equipment. Come back and sit down in comfort."

"Those charts are very helpful, Mr. Sterling," Balthazar said. "We're also interested in real estate here. Who is the most knowledgeable agent?"

Both the Sterlings started to laugh. "I'm sorry,"

Josh said, "it's just that there *isn't* any real estate agent in town. There's a man here in charge of this development—you can see his sign next door. But someone with listings for the area—no. We had a funny experience with that when we first arrived. We'd see signs on houses saying they were for rent or sale, but often there was no phone number. And we thought we were just using the wrong Spanish term for agent, you see. Often a Spanish dictionary doesn't help in Puerto Rico. We had to ask Panama at the restaurant who owned what. Well, everybody here knows who has what, and you'd starve to death selling land in Loiza. Of course, there are some large plots up near the main highway, and they're listed with brokers in San Juan. But let me think, who around here—?"

"Serena will know, dear," Felicity broke in.

"That's right. And she's coming tonight. She's really been investigating the beach area. She's thinking of moving her flock here."

Felicity smiled at Balthazar's puzzled expression. "Serena Burns. You might have heard her name. She's a very famous woman minister in California. She's interested in founding a new community for her followers."

A picture in an airplane magazine came to Balthazar's mind. A tall Valkyrie of a woman in a white robe standing in a glass cathedral with sunlight streaming on golden hair braided around her head. "Yes, I think so," he said. "She's looking at large pieces of land, then?"

"Oh, yes," Felicity answered. "She's very successful."

"She should be," her husband added with a grin. "She's the apostle to the rich."

"Serena is sincere," Felicity hastened to add. "After all, the old and wealthy need solace, too. Of course, they can pay for it. Money solves some of our earthly problems."

"I find her timing interesting," Balthazar said. "Do you think it might have some connection with these bodies?"

"I don't think so, Lieutenant," Felicity said thoughtfully. "As I remember, the first of these five bodies turned up in October. Right? Serena only had her vision a month ago in January. She called me right away because—"

"Her vision?"

"Yes." Felicity nodded soberly. "Her philosophy is complex, but she believes that we have all lost touch with our beginnings, our earliest beginnings in the sea and our first ventures on the earth. Through meditation and massage, particularly of the soles of the feet, she believes we can cure many of our physical and psychic illnesses. To do that, we must go barefoot part of the day—be in contact with the ground itself, and we should wade daily in the sea as well. Of course, she needs a warm climate for that, given the age of most of her followers. She called to say that her nature spirits spoke to her and warned that she and her believers were assimilating too much stress from the ground in California."

Sterling's laugh was more of a whoop. "You mean she needed to expand and the high price of California real estate was giving Serena stress."

Felicity shook her head at her husband, and continued seriously. "Serena is a fascinating blend of the practical and the metaphysical. You can see what I mean," she appealed to Balthazar and Sixto. "Massage is very good for older people's hands and feet. It helps those with arthritis, and it relaxes as well. So many of her beliefs are very good for her followers. She puts them in a comfortable and controlled environment. Meals are nutritious—and a lot of older people, even though they can well afford it, don't bother to eat properly. She allows two glasses of wine with lunch and two with dinner. Alcohol in moderation is a good tranquilizer, but there's a growing problem with older people slipping into alcoholism. She combines attention to their physical needs with a warm and comforting message about the hereafter. There is no place for guilt in her thinking. I have known a great many older people slip into depression, blaming themselves for their children's problems or just regretting things they themselves did in the past."

"I can't help teasing Serena a bit," Josh interjected, "but she's a very shrewd woman. Her 'religion,' if you can call it that, doesn't really contradict any of the faiths these people grew up with. It's vaguely Eastern, but not strange enough to make them uneasy. Many of the rich in our society made their money themselves. They worked hard, and many never had time for study. And I agree with 'Liss, Serena is absolutely convinced that what she is doing is truly helpful. And when she takes my hand and looks at me with her sapphire-blue eyes, I almost believe it myself."

"You are sure that her interest in this particular area only goes back a month or so?" Balthazar persisted. "If someone here knew that an American group with a lot of capital was coming in—you can see my point. Perhaps, the idea was evolving slowly, and she only mentioned it to you recently, but others knew . . . ."

"Given the fact that Serena doesn't think in a straight line," Felicity responded softly, "anything is possible. I've known her for years; we studied for our graduate degrees together. But I'm rather sure Puerto Rico was a recent decision. I talked to her at Christmas and she certainly wasn't consciously thinking of moving anywhere then."

"And," her husband added, "she had quite an offer from a California land developer for her present property in early January. I think that he was one of the nature spirits."

"I was the one who suggested that she look at this particular area." Felicity rose and refilled Sixto's glass. He blushed. "I'm sure she hadn't heard of it before we moved here. But she'd never even been here until last month. She stayed with us then. She was pleased with the location—so near the airport," Felicity continued, "and especially with what she referred to as the atmosphere. When she was here in January, she looked at a few pieces of land, and she is talking to a San Juan firm. She's been very happy with the prices, I gather."

"They are reasonable," Josh nodded. He poured himself another glass of wine and held it up to the light. "And so are the wages for the gardeners, maids, nurses, and everything else she needs. We're also quite close to the University of Puerto Rico's teaching hospital in Carolina."

"Do you know which pieces of land she's interested in?"

Felicity glanced at Josh. "So far just west of the river, I think," he responded. "In the *Piñones*—she was fascinated by that area. But there of course, one is going to have problems with the road for some time."

"Has she ever mentioned land owned by a Mrs. deDiego to the east?"

"No, I don't think so." Felicity frowned. "A large plot for sale near here?"

"Well, a large plot, but as for it being for sale. . . ." Balthazar told them briefly about Emily deDiego.

Felicity's dark eyes were troubled when he finished.

"Josh, that poor woman! She could even have a case of incipient Alzheimer's Disease. Perhaps we could—"

"Now, 'Liss," he warned. "E-checkbook! Serena will be here soon and that seems enough right now."

"You are right, my dear." She looked at the two men. "We don't mean to talk in code. It's just that we realized some time ago that we have an emotional checkbook as well as a financial one. In the past, we've often overdrawn both. One wants to help others, but we can't let them drain either of our accounts."

"Believe me, Felicity," Josh said earnestly, "that woman would be an enormous problem."

"But maybe her property would interest Serena. We could look at it with her. Or just tell her about it."

Josh said nothing.

As they were leaving, the Sterlings apologized for not being more helpful in terms of concrete information on the finding of the bodies. "Josh always swims early, of course, but none of the bodies was ever found on our stretch here. And he swims quite a distance, but I don't think he'd particularly notice anything on the shore. I often walk on the beach, but that's later in the day."

She pointed to where the street ended at the water's edge. "But then, too, you notice, there are three streetlights right on our corner. Not a good choice of a place if you preferred darkness. At one time, some years ago, *Playa Del Mar* was intended to be quite an extensive development. It was never finished. But," she shrugged philosophically, "a lot of things are unfinished in Loiza. Or if they are," she gestured down the beach to the mayor's project, "there is always an element of wonder. In that case, one wonders why such an elaborate pavilion was not built near a better road, or in an area with more parking." There was an impish gleam in her dark eyes.

16

IT WAS HOT, and away from the beach's constant light breeze the air felt heavy on the skin. Balthazar sat, waiting for Sixto, in the confiscated car that Terron had provided. It was a late-model Buick, painted deep purple with pale lavender velour seat coverings. In New York, or in Puerto Rico, it was recognizably a pimp-mobile. Extra chrome, now pitted by the salt air, had been piled on. It had electric windows, an electric sunroof, and every conceivable gadget on the dash-board. But the radio's retractable aerial had a quirky tendency to shoot up on its own volition, and the air conditioning no longer worked.

They were parked half on the sidewalk, or what could be regarded as a sidewalk, on a labyrinthine street jammed with dilapidated houses. Each house shared a common wall with the next, and all crowded up to the edge of the sidewalk. Heads had been turning all day at the sight of the car, and even now Balthazar had the uncomfortable sensation of being stared at, but the only person he could see was a slender black boy seated cross-legged about four feet away from him on a porch. Whenever Balthazar looked at him, he turned away self-consciously.

It was the fourth time they'd stopped, and Sixto had gone again to ask for the whereabouts of a woman named Lorena Garcia who had discovered one of the corpses. She lived in a tumble-down shack on the beach, but she had not been there when they arrived that

124

morning. A man walking by thought she was staying with a daughter in Loíza.

Balthazar scowled and wiped his forehead. He knew what Lorena Garcia would say when she was found. *"No se, Señor,"* or *"No se, Oficial,"* or just *"No se."* "I don't know." All afternoon they had heard a steady chorus of *"No se."* Some of these old people were uneasy, some were surly, most were frightened, but they all said the same thing in answer to his and Sixto's questions. Except for those who just shook their heads or shrugged.

Balthazar was frustrated, tired, and grumpy. It was like playing Fish, a game he had not liked even as a child. You had to collect four cards of the same number. You asked another player for the one you wanted. If he didn't have it, he replied, "Go fish," and you drew from the face-down pool of cards before you. Soon you had a large collection of cards in your hand, too many to hold, and you had to keep them hidden. Sometimes you had painstakingly acquired three and then another player drew one from the pool and gleefully collected all of yours. You never knew who held the needed cards.

Sixto got back in the car, leaving the door open in the hope of a passing breeze, lifted his thick hair from his forehead with spread fingers and then shook his head. "Señora Garcia's son-in-law says at the moment she is visiting a friend. He does not know when she will return. He even seemed to hope that she would never return."

In irritation, Balthazar said, "There is no point in this. None. This case cannot be solved by two outsiders. If it can be solved at all. We should put on trunks and go to the beach."

"Sí," said Sixto, glumly.

"Nobody even cares whether it is solved, except for those people who are scared, and they don't think we can be of any help. If we were in San Juan, we could have some organization, and some men working on it, and you could at least eliminate some of the possibilities. There we'd have the street people who know and a few who would talk. Villareal could get the information we need on boats and who was where when and. . . ."

Sixto started to smile. And so did Balthazar. They were both imagining San Juan's Chief of Homicide, Herman Villareal, with his near-fanatic dedication to procedure, to checking fingerprints and ballistics reports, caught up in a search like this one. He'd react like a maddened bee, Balthazar thought, stinging a pane of glass.

"Still," Balthazar complained, "this investigation makes typing reports in triplicate seem an intelligent exercise. We have to get information on land values from a woman preacher from California and maps of the coast from a jewelry designer. Speaking of that, Sixto, did you notice what kind of maps Sterling had under the one he showed us?"

"No."

"They looked like tax district maps, property tax. They would indicate who would own what piece of property."

"Perhaps he had them for the. . . ." Sixto stopped, trying to think of a Spanish word for a woman minister and gave up. "For the señora who preaches."

"Maybe. But you'll notice he didn't seem anxious to show them to us. That's why I asked for real estate information. I wondered if he'd volunteer those maps. But he didn't. What kind of business was he in before taking up jewelry design? Loiza is an odd place for them to choose to live, although they make it sound logical."

"They return in the fall, no? The bodies began to appear then, too." Sixto exhanged a grin with the little boy sitting on the porch.

"And they have this friend with an odd religion who could very well be a woman con artist. Is she making sure that her followers leave her their money, instead of willing it to their children?"

"Perhaps," Sixto said slowly, "but the rubbing of the old people's feet, giving them good food, making them happy. That is not so bad." He wondered if his mother would be happy in Serena's care. But then his mother was a devout Catholic, and it was difficult to imagine her complacently eating food someone else had prepared. She'd be out in the kitchen telling the beleaguered cook how to do it properly.

"In any case, the Burns woman's plans to buy land here now seems as if it ought to have something to do with this. But what?"

They sat in silence for some time. The little boy had slipped down from the porch and was timidly studying the car's sleek hood ornament—a flying, bare-breasted woman.

"Why would anyone want to kill us, Sixto? We don't *know* anything. We've been stumbling around like idiots in the dark since we got here. So we've asked a lot of questions about a lot of different things. Terron and his men did, too. No one tried to kill them. Do you think we might have been mistaken? The moon was shining on the bus's windshield and we couldn't really see inside. If the driver was himself black and wearing black clothing . . . it could have happened the way Terron said."

"*Sí.*"

"We only have to stay here for three more days. We could go around and ask a few more questions, but we don't have to push it. Then we explain to headquarters that it's really a case for the Loiza men. Which is what we thought in the first place." Balthazar drummed his fingers distractedly on the dashboard. "The people here *are* really frightened."

"*Sí.*"

"But Terron is a competent man. Perhaps a little close to the problem."

"*Sí.*"

"But that school bus, Sixto. Someone getting desperate. It wouldn't have been hard. Anybody who wanted to know where we were could have found that out. And that is the only road back to Loiza. The moon was bright. He just waits on the top of that little rise before the bridge and he can see us coming a long way off. He could get us anywhere along those walls. Just shove us into the concrete—head-on. Think that's what happened?"

"*Sí*," said Sixto grimly, starting the car.

"So do I. And I don't believe in ghosts that go fishing. Let's go find Señora Garcia."

The rutted pathway was clearly not intended for cars, particularly large, low-slung American cars. The Buick's purple hood dipped down like the prow of a boat in choppy waters, then bounced up again. Balthazar and Sixto were bumped and jostled, despite the fact that the speedometer needle was only jittering between the ten and fifteen mile-an-hour marks.

Both sides of the sandy road were scattered with debris: plastic bottles, broken glass, rusted nails, and here and there a soiled diaper, a solitary shoe, a squashed hat. It was as if a group of careless children, hurrying somewhere, had discarded their clothing and their possessions piece by piece. The road narrowed to a footpath which led to an old house. In back of that, one could see other ramshackle buildings.

The sagging fence surrounding the house had been made by winding old wire around uneven boards and pieces of driftwood. The yard was crammed with what seemed a whole flea market's unsaleable items. In one corner there was a three-legged table, a backless chair, a rusted box spring, and a car seat with most of the stuffing gone; another had a pile of stacked wood of all lengths and kinds. There were old tires and car parts scattered everywhere. Chickens squawked and scurried through the rubbish. On the side of the house, an ancient donkey tied to a tree eyed them somnolently.

The house itself had originally been made of wood, but wherever a graying board had split or broken, it had been patched with pieces of flattened tin. On the porch stood a doorless refrigerator, now stuffed with multicolored rags. Next to it leaned a rocking chair, its cane bottom in shreds. The house and yard could easily have been put down anywhere in the impoverished rural

American South, Balthazar thought, as he got out of the car. He felt a long way from Manhattan.

Even before they reached the gate, they could hear the woman's angry voice, pouring out a torrent of reproach. She was speaking in Spanish, but she spoke so rapidly, and without ever pausing for breath, that Balthazar felt that he was listening to a prima donna singing an imcomprehensible Italian aria. They could hear a man's ineffectual pleadings, a barely audible counterpart. That, the nature of her complaints, and her impressive lung power heightened the impression of the solo of a betrayed operatic soprano. The two men stopped at the gate.

". . . the hurt in my heart and she, an old friend of my mother's, and a friend of my own. I say a friend, but no friend could act—"

"But Momée doesn't mean—" the man's voice quavered.

". . . taken her bottles of cider and although that is not expensive what can she expect from me, a woman whose son, having a good job at a service station, gives her not one penny because he has a selfish wife, and this old woman and I have drunk the cider that I brought and, holding each other, have wept over these children of ours, her son so far away in the city of Boston and never coming home although I know he sends her money that she does not tell me of because she is afraid that I will not send my friends, and I have other friends, there are many people who would call Lorena Garcia their *dear* friend, who are happy to say they know—"

"Lorena, you must understand—" the man tried feebly to interrupt.

"And you, Junior, who was also my friend, I thought, and did I not send to you also the man who needed a token arranged because his enemy wished him harm, you, the only person this stubborn old woman would listen to, would not take my part, even though I have stored the Voodoo drums in my house and that was, after all, a favor, you would not insist that I must have a part in the ceremony because, although I have not the training of a mambo, what matter is that and the old man from Haiti would not know because I would not disgrace myself or her or anyone else because I am a woman who knows always how to conduct herself which everyone knows and only jealousy on that old woman's part . . ."

"But people will hear you, Lorena, and you must not talk so loudly of the ceremony or—"

". . . and so people ought to know, to know how Momée is excluding me and who could hear me in any case except old Albin, and he should know what I am saying, even though he does not believe in the *loa* or how could he wander about alone, sharpening knives, no home, but he should know what I am saying because then he would never feel sorry for himself that he has no house or children or friends because children and friends squeeze one's heart like a ripe orange and throw away the rind—"

Balthazar and Sixto moved onto the porch and Balthazar cleared his throat in warning before knocking loudly on the broken screen.

The woman did not pause, but they heard a chair scrape against the floorboards and a wizened face peered around the corner through the screen. When the old man saw them, his almost toothless mouth gaped. He hurriedly opened the door and stepped out, his thin chest heaving in fright. At the sound of their voices, the woman's tirade ceased abruptly and one could hear only the rasp of a file somewhere in the back of the tiny house.

In Spanish, Balthazar explained who they were and asked if they could speak with Señora Garcia. Alarmed, the old man stumbled back against the screendoor as if to hold it shut, to conceal the woman's presence.

But she came barging out onto the porch, almost bowling him over, trying to pull her faded blue dress down a little here and there so that it would not stretch so tightly across her enormous breasts, her thick waist, her heavy stomach. A red and white kerchief was tied around her hair and she wore large gold hoop earrings which swung as she stomped forward. She was well past middle age, but no wrinkles seamed her broad black face. Her flat nose merged into round, packed cheeks. The solid flesh of her arms looked like inflated rubber.

She was obviously struggling to regain control of herself, and she compressed her fleshy lips together between her teeth. But the anger still flared in her eyes. "I am Lorena Garcia," she declared truculently.

When Balthazar told her that they wanted to ask her about the corpse on the beach, she glanced uneasily at the old man. His mouth opened and closed, fish-like, but he said nothing. When Balthazar politely asked his name, he had trouble speaking, but at last he gabbled, "Junior Pabon." In answer to Balthazar's two other questions, he responded only with a croaked monosyllable. No. He never went out on the beach at night. No. He knew nothing of the corpses.

The woman was growing increasingly restive, plucking at her earring, and trying to avoid Pabon's eye. When Balthazar turned to her with a smile, she transferred her gaze to their luxurious car. He emphasized how important it was for them to have a knowledgeable person's impressions of the scene where a corpse was found. She admitted reluctantly that she had discovered one of the bodies, although she repeated twice that a young jogger had arrived immediately thereafter. He had thought she should stay there while he called the police. It had been a horrible sight, and she had stood some distance away, only looking over her shoulder occasionally. She had been terribly upset. Sixto shook his head sympathetically, concern in his dark eyes.

She was exactly the person they needed to talk to, Balthazar assured her. He apologized for keeping the Señora standing. He gestured toward the car she had been eying so avidly and asked if they could take her to her home.

The old man watched them mutely as they walked

off. He was obviously glad she was leaving, but the sight of her escorts distressed him.

Holding the backseat car door open for her, Balthazar helped her as she clumsily settled herself, glancing about the lavender interior with approbation. He walked around the car and climbed in next to her. Sixto started the car and guided it majestically around the ravine-like ruts.

Señora Garcia enthusiastically elaborated on the terror she felt on seeing the dead man's face. His eyes had been shut but she could see instantly that he was dead. His face was shrunken and there was the hole, very ugly, in his temple. She described how the corpse was dressed, and stated, many times, that she was sure she had never seen him before, and that she hoped never again to have such an experience. It upset her so much that she'd had to move in with her daughter.

Balthazar stressed the value of her information, and told her how long they had been looking for her, and that many of their informants had noted that she would be able to tell them, to help them understand the meaning of this crime that had been terrifying the whole community.

She nodded, straightened her kerchief, compressed her lips.

But when Balthazar asked for her explanation, she wriggled uncomfortably. She burst out that she would suffer bad luck to the end of her days for even talking about such things. Balthazar murmured that the spirits worked in many ways, that they might be taking this opportunity to let the police know the situation so that the police would not interfere.

By the time they reached her daughter's house, the woman had told them only that there would be a Voodoo ceremony this Friday in the rain forest. She indicated that she thought that it had something to do with the bodies found on the beach, but it was not her responsibility to talk about it. She herself was going to attend, of course, but she had been excluded from the planning and active participation. Some people, whom she did not care to name, thought they were better than

others who, they asserted, lacked "training." She would
be much blamed if she said anything more.

Dropping her voice, and looking carefully through
all the open car windows, she told them that Momée
Molina was the woman they needed to speak to. She
was the one who was so important, or thought she was.
Begrudgingly she gave them directions to the Molina
house, but added that since it was now almost dark,
they would not find her tonight. No, it was not possible. There had been a death in the community that day.
Naturally, Momée was busy. Funerals were always held
at four o'clock the afternoon following a death. Surely
they knew that. Momée would be very busy. She said
she would say no more. This time she closed her lips.
And she said no more.

17

"T ERRON PROBABLY WASN'T KIDDING—a *horse* is the ideal way to get back to these places," Balthazar said. The morning breeze was cool now, but this road was no better. The Buick hit a deep pothole filled with sand, and both men grazed their heads on its roof.

"If you grow up in San Juan," Sixto said with a sigh, smoothing his hair back in place while keeping his eye on the narrow road, "the only horses you see are on the signs outside the betting office. There are a lot of those. I do not know how to ride a horse. I am a policeman, not a cowboy."

"Anyway, our list from Terron is getting shorter. We can talk to this Momée Molina, and if the Garcia woman is right, she's in charge of the Voodoo ceremony they're having. And the reason they're having the ceremony has to be relevant." He paused. "Well, it doesn't *have* to be."

"No, but it is possible," Sixto said. "These people think they know why the bodies appear. And we do not."

"Right, and I want to at least hear their theory. It may help us."

"If they will tell us their theory." Sixto sounded discouraged.

They climbed out of the car. Seeing the woman ahead of them sitting on an old folding chair, her huge body overlapping its sides but her back straight, Balthazar was not encouraged either. At the sight of them, she hastily slipped whatever she was working on into a crumpled brown paper bag by her side.

The tiny house behind her held at most two rooms. Once a bright red, its color had long ago faded. Next to it leaned a sagging outhouse with bleached bits of driftwood carefully nailed over the gaps in its rotting sides. The buildings stood on the edge of a large, tree-crowded field a hundred yards from the beach. In the near distance, one could see the tall pines that surrounded the Sterling house.

The old woman stood up as they approached, watching them. She was nearing seventy, but her thick body was upright. She looked at the two men steadily and unsmilingly. She said she was Momée Molina. When they asked her about the bodies found on the beaches, she promptly informed them that she knew nothing.

"Then why are you arranging this ceremony on Friday in the rain forest?" Balthazar asked her bluntly.

Her tiny, bright eyes blinked, and the slackening of her body expressed intense dismay. "Who tells you that this is true?"

When they did not answer, she waved her hand dismissingly. "Some ignorant person. And this is no business of the *Policía*."

"You must let us decide that," Balthazar said firmly. "We know that you hope to end the appearance of these bodies by your ritual. Why not tell us why you think this person is doing it?"

"You no understand," she replied stiffly.

"Is it his intention to frighten people?" he persisted.

"You no understand," she repeated stubbornly.

They heard a loud rustling and a pretty, light-skinned black girl, who certainly looked sixteen but might have been younger, came around the side of the house, dragging a heavy palm frond behind her. Her dark hair was pulled back in a neat waistlength braid and there were drops of perspiration on her forehead, her upper lip. Sweat had stained the armpits of her clinging melodramatic yellow t-shirt. She dropped the branch quickly, wiped her hands on her jeans, and brushed her forehead with the back of her arm. She could not meet Balthazar's eyes, but she smiled shyly at Sixto. Returning her smile, Sixto mentioned that the color of her shirt made her skin glow. She tittered, put her hand over her lips, and lowered her eyes.

"Leave that," the old woman said sharply. "It is too heavy for you. Go back and gather some green coconuts now."

"But you *said*—" the girl began defensively. There was a touch of exasperation in her soft voice.

"Go," the woman said, hardly moving her lips.

"Your granddaughter?" Balthazar asked pleasantly.

"*Sí.*"

"What is your name?" Sixto asked smiling, moving a little nearer. He had once told Balthazar that he never felt shy with girls under eighteen, but if they were any older, his tongue could not leave his teeth.

"Ana," she replied, glancing at him and then looking down again, nibbling her lower lip.

"Do your parents live here, too?"

"Oh, no," she said. "In Boston. This summer I'm going to. . . ."

"Don't chatter, child," her grandmother interrupted.

"But Momée, how can I do what you tell me if you keep changing your mind?" Ana clearly resented being called a child. "Did you forget that you *just* told me it was necessary to have burnt palm branches?" She spoke with affection and what sounded like a faint edge of mockery. How often the young address their elders in that tone, Balthazar thought. Perhaps the gentle ridicule was a shield against the power of the adult and the knowledge of their own dependence.

"*I* will help," Sixto volunteered enthusiastically. "Show me where the palm branches are."

"Do not bother the *Policía*," Momée said sternly.

But the girl did not respond to the warning. She pointed toward the eastern edge of the field, and sprinted off, giggling. Sixto dashed after her, and as he caught up to her, she began talking animatedly. Bending his head close to hers, he was obviously listening with interest. Momée looked after them and her eyes were unreadable. She shrugged off all of Balthazar's persistent questions. Finally, with an imperious, dismissive wave, she disappeared into the house and closed the door.

Sixto was anxiously examining his gun, holding it out the car window in the fading twilight, checking to see if sand had gotten in the barrel. He was proud of his new .357 Magnum. They had pulled over some distance up the road.

"Logically," Balthazar said, "the next stop is another visit with old Junior. But I have the feeling he isn't going to be at home. I could tell from the old woman's expression when I tried to rattle her by mentioning we were also going to talk to him. Too bad the girl didn't know more. . . . Pretty girl."

"Sí." Sixto carefully rubbed the handle of the gun with his handkerchief. "Very pretty. But too young."

"You can see why her grandmother keeps her way out there and eyes her like a bomb about to explode."

Sixto raised an eyebrow. "She said she goes with her grandmother on the beach at night sometimes, because her grandmother does not feel it is safe for anyone to go out alone."

"She say why?"

"The gray pigs are out at night. She also called them another name but I did not hear it properly. They walk in columns and. . . ."

"These are people?"

"Sí. I think. Bad ones. If they run into you alone at night, you either have to join their group or they do terrible things to you. They can turn you into an animal, Ana says. That's why the veterinarians are always sticking needles into the cows on the dairy farms. To make sure they are cows and not people."

"You can see where that comes from. Sometimes animals get the most intelligent looks in their eyes. I had a dog that looked as if he understood everything I

said. He always seemed impressed by what he heard
. . . well, what else?"

"There is also a car with strange headlights that
comes . . . takes you away. You never come back. She
and her grandmother have heard it at night."

"You have to admit, Sixto, that the Voodoo people
have an idea there. In cold climates, everybody—
including the young—has to stay in to keep warm. Here
you scare them into staying home. The old people
really believe it themselves, so they're convincing. Otherwise, the young would be running around half the
night doing God knows what. . . . I take that back, God
knows precisely what they'd do and so do we."

"Ana would get into trouble." Sixto paused, looking slightly shocked. "She told me a story . . . and she is
not yet fifteen!"

"Girls raised in the country are pretty straightforward," Balthazar said, remembering a farm girl he'd
met at summer camp when he was twelve.

"That girl . . . she said that on the night of the full
moon before Christmas, she and her grandmother are
out gathering plants in a field. Her grandmother is at
the other end digging. Ana looks out on the beach and
sees the old man who sharpens knives leading his donkey
by the halter. Albin, *sí*? Tied on the donkey's back are
two big rolls under a blanket. She is very curious. What
can be under the blanket? She stands very still and
watches him."

Sixto shook his head disapprovingly. "You understand that Ana is a nice girl. Not some street *chiquita*.
And she is giggling when she tells me this! They are
watermelons!"

Sixto replaced the gun in the holster strapped to his
boot, started the car, and edged forward slowly down
the bumpy road.

Balthazar waited. Sixto said nothing. He was still
shaking his head, his lips pursed.

"Well? What about the watermelons?"

"*Baltasar*, when I was young, the girls in my
classes at the Catholic school would never . . . The

young these days. . . ." He flicked on the headlights, his mouth almost prim.

"Sixto, what does he *do* with the watermelons?"

"She is laughing very, very hard when she tells me. I am, of course very . . . *surprised*. Who could imagine doing *that* to a watermelon? And she sees my face, laughs some more, puts her hands up and says, 'Well, his donkey is a male.' "

18

"I THINK it's the little green olives," Balthazar said pensively as they drove toward Rio Grande, the sweet smell of the dew-fresh grass drifting in through the car window. "Absolutely delicious chicken stew, but the stroke of culinary genius on your mother's part is adding those stuffed olives to that light tomato sauce." He was remembering the casserole they'd had for dinner the evening before at their unit in the vacation center. They were both hungry for breakfast now, but Panama didn't open until 7:00 A.M. They'd decided that dawn might be the best time for impromptu interviews with the early rising old people who often checked the beach each morning for wood and usable items thrown up by the sea.

"*Sí*, but the cabbage is important," Sixto considered. "It adds to the sauce flavor and . . . um . . . something."

"Funny, I wouldn't have thought I'd like cabbage in a chicken stew. But then I never realized I was a custard fanatic, either. I ate a whole quarter of that cream-cheese flan. It's so smooth, and that good caramel sauce on top." He sniffed the delightful air, savoring the beautiful morning. His senses seemed as finely-tuned as a child's and as alive.

"If we park," he continued, "across from the little river that borders Emily deDiego's land, and walked away from the country club toward the Sterlings' house, we might catch the owners of those shacks that are on the beach but aren't on any road. If they haven't all moved into town already." Balthazar rubbed his knee and wondered if it were up to the mile and a half walk on the sand. Perhaps if he stayed on the firm sand near the shoreline. . . .

Pulling just off the road, Sixto climbed out and shivered in the first rays of pale sunlight. He took the gun from his boot holster and tucked in the back of his pants under his loose shirt. Observing him, Balthazar did the same, recalling that in Puerto Rico, all guns, including those carried by the police, must be concealed.

Stretching expansively, Balthazar wiggled his leg back and forth. His knee felt good even without a swim, but he gazed wistfully at the dark blue wind-ruffled sea, ignoring the detritus of seaweed, plastic bottles, and uprooted tree trunks on the edges. Above, two small white terns were blown across the peach-colored sky. Suddenly, Sixto, who had been walking briskly to the shore, broke into a run. "Hurry," he called loudly without turning. As Balthazar dashed forward, he could see that what lay on the water's edge was not a large piece of dark driftwood. It was a partially submerged body.

The face was in the sand, the bony, bare, black arms outstretched with curving fingers as if the dead man were desperately trying to purchase a hold on the sand. The brown foaming surf swirled around the bare feet as if trying to drag the body into the sea.

Each grabbing one of the toothpick-thin upper arms, they pulled the corpse farther up on the shore. Sixto knelt and turned it over carefully. At the sight of the face, he grimaced and Balthazar involuntarily jerked his own head back, glad that he'd had no breakfast. Chunks of skin had been ripped from the cheeks, exposing yellow molars. The lips were pulled back, and the mouth seemed to be literally grinning from ear to ear. Both the eyes and the eyelids had been gouged out, the white bone below them exposed. There was no gray in the dark, close-cropped hair, but the scalp showed through in coin-sized patches. Centered in the forehead was a small hole with jagged edges.

The once white shirt was covered with slimy ribbons of seaweed. The gray polyester pants were ripped, stained, and sodden. Several of the toes were missing, and the rest were stripped of flesh.

Swallowing hard, Sixto pulled down the shirt collar and pointed to a rough incision in the base of the neck. "Embalmed," he noted tersely. "That is where they insert the embalming fluid tube." He reached down to roll up one of the corpse's trouser legs.

"Shouldn't we wait for the photographer?" Balthazar asked, putting one index finger gingerly next to the bullet hole to judge its size.

"In Puerto Rico," Sixto answered, inching up the sopping pants leg, "detectives are technically coroners. We are supposed to establish the cause of death, if possible. In this case, of course," he grunted as he tugged on the material, "I just want to be sure of the embalming."

"You take special classes to be able to do that?"

Sixto rolled his eyes. "No. On-the-job training with a more experienced officer." The young man had now found another incision on the inside of the skinny thigh. "They put the embalming fluid in the neck, and the blood comes out of the femoral artery here." Frowning, he stood up, brushing his hands fiercely as if to clean them of more than sand. "The experts will have to decide what he died of the first time."

"And if, I suppose, the corpse was actually floating in the sea or if this damage was done by shore predators. The file indicates that the others had only been in the water briefly. Well, if our culprit wants to make sure the corpse is found on a specific beach, he wouldn't throw it in the sea. Might be carried out too far. If he's familiar with the tides around here, he could leave them near the edge, though." He straightened up. "That's either a .22 or .25 caliber hole. Too small for a .38."

He considered. "First chance we've had to be on the spot. If there are any jeep or four-wheeler tracks on the edges of that field, we need to keep them from being disturbed. But the damn car has no radio"—he eyed the

crumbling facade of the deDiego house across the river—
"and the Senora has no telephone wires leading to her
house."

"I can watch," Sixto's eyes flicked quickly over the
corpse, "and still check near the field for tracks. You
report to the Loiza station." Inwardly wincing at the
idea of twisting his knee while slogging through the deep
loose sand by the trees, Balthazar nodded in agreement.

"I'll find some coffee." He trudged back to the car,
taking care to follow his own footsteps. But the wind
seemed to be erasing all their tracks, even the deeper
hoof marks of the cattle that occasionally wandered out
of the palm fields.

Sixto glanced again at the corpse's grotesquely grinning face and yelled, "Coffee only!"

A jeep, or even a dune buggy, could easily have
woven between the palm trees, Sixto mused, checking
the border of the field, although the size of the dead
fronds on the ground and the volunteers sprouting from
fallen coconuts would seem to make it impassable in a
car. He was almost fifty yards from the corpse and
absorbed in studying the sand. Dozens of little crabs
dived for their holes as he approached, leaving hiero-
glyphics in the soft surface. Even a city person could
recognize a nice clear tire track, but he wondered if the
people here could actually follow a person's trail as the
old Indians were said to do. The trouble with this entire
case, he reflected, was that he and the Lieutenant were
from the city. On the other hand, in the Strangler case,
the Lieutenant had just arrived in Puerto Rico and still
managed to solve that case brilliantly. Sometimes, he'd
said, being an outsider was an advantage. And, Sixto
thought, this time too, the Lieutenant would be able. . . .
Looking back over his shoulder, he was alarmed to find
the tide was now surging again around the feet of the
corpse.

He ran back and was about to grasp one of the
fragile arms when the sickening notion occurred to him

that it might pull loose from the body. Bending over the head, he reached under the armpits to drag the corpse forward. The mutilated face was close to his own, and his stomach lurched. That dreadful inhuman smile. He squinched his eyes shut, slipping his hands under the body. No wonder that fat Senora had—

"Evil," said a voice in guttural Spanish close behind him.

Sixto jerked upright and wheeled around. The impassive face of Manuel, the deDiego's caretaker, stared into his own.

"Wh . . . where did you come from?"

Manuel pointed impassively to some thick-trunked pines near the palm field.

"I didn't see you. How long have you been here? Did you see anyone before we arrived?"

Manual shook his head almost imperceptibly. "Horse loose. I look. See you by field. You run back here. I come, too."

"Manuel, Manuel!" Emily deDiego's high-pitched voice quavered. She was standing on the edge of the shallow river, holding up the edge of her dress almost daintily as she prepared to wade across. Her gray hair had come loose from its bun, and she kept ineffectually brushing the wind-blown strands from her eyes. "Who are you talking to? Feel him. Feel him. Is he real?"

"Señora no should come." Manuel gestured with his thick cane, and moved as quickly as he could toward her. Splashing through the water, he took her arm with an almost courtly hold and led her back toward the house. With pity in his dark eyes, Sixto watched them move slowly across the sand.

"Another one?" Velez ruffled his hair, his troubled eyes darting around the empty station room. "Sergeant Terron's not here. But"—he reached for the phone— "I'll call Carolina headquarters. That's what we did before. They send out photographers and a crew and

. . . a body wagon. I suppose they'll take it to San Juan like the others."

"I'd like Sergeant Terron to see this," Balthazar said. "He could tell us if this particular one differs in any way from the others. Could you reach him first, please?"

Velez checked his watch. "The Sergeant is having breakfast now."

"Could you call him at home?" Balthazar asked wearily.

"He isn't at home. He'll be at Panama's."

"Call Carolina. I'll catch Terron at Panama's." Balthazar headed for the stairs.

"Oh, Lieutenant," Velez hollered after him. "Would you tell Cardenas his mother phoned? He's supposed to call her."

As Balthazar reached the door of the restaurant, the cook, a short, square Puerto Rican woman carrying a pile of plastic shopping bags, threw open the screen door and banged right into him. She'd been looking back over her shoulder, calling out that she was off to the native market in Canovanas. Smiling shyly and apologetically at the detective, she bustled over to an old pickup truck with crumpled fenders.

He caught the screendoor before it shut and closed it quietly behind him. The restaurant looked empty, although he could smell the welcome aroma of fresh coffee.

"I tell you, the mayor said nothing when they were here. Nothing sensible. I made sure that I explained his ideas for their benefit so his mind wouldn't wander off onto that subject." Panama's voice, tinged with worry, came from the back room. Through the thick vines, Balthazar could see her sitting across from Terron, who was chewing stolidly on a piece of toast.

She nervously clicked her polished fingernails on the edge of her coffee cup. "Couvertier hasn't seen either of those two from San Juan again, he says. We don't know if that idea has even occurred to him. And now he's off for two days to the Mayors' Conference in Ponce."

"For all the way he talks, man's not stupid. But he could mess it up for us. Only hope I've got for any money, *mi cariño*, and if you want to live in the mountains when we get married. . . ." Terron reached forward and took her small hand. "The doctor said my mother will not survive this time. Matter of days. I was at the hospital until late last night, and she never opened her eyes. As soon as your divorce is final—"

Balthazar turned back, opened the door quietly, and thumped it shut. "Panama?" he raised his voice. She hurried around the divider, her smile welcoming but uneasy.

"Come for breakfast?"

He shook his head, but before he could ask for the sergeant, Terron came forward, his hat under his arm, wiping his mustache with a napkin.

"I'll get you some coffee," Panama said, throwing a questioning glance at Terron.

"Two, please. To go," Balthazar said. He described the discovery of the latest corpse to Terron, studying his face. The sergeant's left eye was almost shut. Perhaps, Balthazar thought, fatigue weakened the lid. Terron's right eye widened slightly in his stoic face. Throwing his napkin on a nearby table in disgust, he strode back toward the kitchen. "Panama, make us some ham sandwiches, too, would you?"

Jamming his hat on his head, he brushed by Balthazar. "I'll go call in on the jeep radio. Follow you out there. One way or another, this'll eat up the whole damned day." The screen door banged loudly behind him. Balthazar watched him stride to the blue and white jeep, interested in Terron's lack of reaction.

19

"SOME SOULS are sent back to this life fairly quickly because they are needed. Wise souls, who can help others," Serena Burns was saying in her musical, calm voice.

She was holding Balthazar's right hand and gently and expertly massaging it. Instead of feeling awkward, he was astonishingly relaxed. He was thinking how good his hand felt—it was a wonderful sensation. He had never before thought about a hand, all by itself, feeling pleased.

Given what they'd been told by Felicity Sterling, Balthazar was skirting the question of why Serena had decided to move, but he was interested in finding out when she had first had the idea, and with whom she had discussed it. Serena's idea of answering a straightforward question, however, often involved roaming through several reincarnations. She had two other disconcerting habits. She believed touching people—even recent acquaintances—aided communication. And she sounded immensely sensible discussing ideas he would otherwise have thought implausible.

"I told Felicity right away, of course," she said thoughtfully, looking at the ocean through the Sterling's veranda screens. "She is an old soul. I don't think she herself quite accepts the extent to which she and I are in constant spiritual communion. We have spent all of our previous lifetimes together, sometimes as sisters. The problem is that souls like hers are terribly open to the

147

stress of existence. They don't remember the lessons of other lifetimes consciously, but this information is lodged in their imaginations. So they empathize very readily with other people. They are extremely sensitive to atmosphere, too."

Balthazar was thinking that his left hand quite consciously also wanted a massage. Serena picked it up and began gently kneading the base of his palm. "Felicity was wise to leave the pressures of university life. People there are surprisingly prejudiced. She is a woman and they consider her a black. She was very concerned because Josh, too, was under a great deal of business stress. But I can sense their content here in Loiza."

Serena smiled directly at Balthazar. She was a stunningly beautiful woman in her late forties. Her eyes were nearly violet, with dark lashes, and there was only the faintest tracery of wrinkles on a face haloed by golden braids wound loosely around her head. She wore a white silk dress whose loose folds minimized her considerable height. "Balthazar. A wonderful name. One of the three wise men," she murmured, her luminous eyes on his face.

He cleared his throat. "When did you tell your community about the need to relocate?"

"Immediately after the spirits spoke to me, over a month ago now. Most of our members—we refer to ourselves as Meditationists—are elderly. They need time to adjust to change, to seek inner guidance about what they want to do. Of course, there is no need for any to leave California. We are going to keep a large condominium building there next to the temple but we will no longer maintain extensive grounds. Here we will have retreat facilities for those who wish to come for short periods, as well as residences for those who wish to stay much of the year."

"I can see that many of your people would have adult children. No doubt they would want to talk this over with them as well," Balthazar observed.

"Yes. Although many of the Meditationists have

already shared their acceptance of the idea of moving with me."

Her strong thumb kneaded the center of his palm. "You are uneasy with that idea. Perhaps you feel I am using undue influence on my people. You have seen one of the first problems I faced in preparing for this move. Many children do not want their parents to move a great distance from them, away from familial support. So I naturally felt that keeping facilities in California would be necessary. But the spirits were, as always, right. My congregation also needs a place that is absolutely anxiety-free. Our loved ones, children and grandchildren, simply because they are loved, often cause stress."

As she rubbed the knuckle on his index finger, Balthazar felt the tension draining from it. "Our philosophy is aimed at dealing with our problems through meditation, and through massage," she continued softly, "but it also calls for eliminating problems where possible. We needed a place that allowed complete peace. As I am sure you know, California had a most turbulent history. Vibrations remain."

"Did you mention Puerto Rico as a possible site to your followers?"

"Oh, no. I specifically asked the congregation *not* to share their feelings with me on the question of a particular place. It would block the spirits' voices. And it might well cause dissension."

Sixto was watching her intently, fascinated. She smiled at him as if she were sure of his complete understanding. "Then, on a practical level, these decisions must be made with the well-being of the entire group in mind, you see. Some might have felt that Mexico, given its proximity, might be a good choice. It would be very economical as well. But there have always been periods of intense political unrest there. There are also a few other disadvantages. There might be problems with land ownership that one would not face here. Besides, Puerto Rico has American standards in regard to the water supply and dairy products. We eat a great deal of yogurt and cheese, as well as fresh fish. Then, too, older people need familiarity in their surroundings. Here we have American products as well as American television."

"Did you discuss any locations with other trusted friends?" Balthazar had to force himself to keep to the subject. He was becoming remarkably drowsy. He and Sixto had spent yesterday afternoon and all morning, in the car and on foot, trying to chase down the elusive occupants of the shacks near the beach where they'd found the corpse.

"No. Only with my lawyer, and of course, that was in confidence. I needed his advice on several matters and I wanted him to find reliable real estate agents in various places."

"He certainly did an excellent job in finding a man here," Felicity said, coming in with a tray. "Here's your favorite sour orange tea, Serena. Josh says he's very pleased with the San Juan realtor's research. Josh is still out with him, but he told me that the man had already looked at the deDiego land and its title is unclouded. I had no idea how much thought Josh had already given to your move here. He even collected some local property maps, doing some research. Of course, he wouldn't tell me, knowing how I worry about his blood pressure if he once again gets involved in property."

"You are looking at the deDiego property?" Balthazar asked.

"More than looking." Serena smiled as Felicity put an exquisite porcelain tea set before her. "And I understand that we have you two to thank for bringing my attention to that particular plot. The spirits must have been speaking to you, too."

"Do you mean that she is willing to sell?"

"Oh not *sell*, Balthazar. I spoke to Emily for a long time yesterday afternoon," Serena said, "and she was quite at peace with our arrangements when I left." She looked at the men tranquilly. "There is no need for her to neglect her husband's last wishes in this matter. But I told her that Luis's spirit was very unquiet because of her unhappiness. So we are not buying her land; she is going to donate it to the community, except for a section near the river which she is giving outright to Manuel, the caretaker. Neither she nor her late husband have any living relatives. In return for her generous gift, Emily's living expenses will be taken care of for her lifetime."

"Perhaps she should not make a hasty decision. She is not a well woman," Balthazar said uneasily.

"No, she is not. And I will take her back with me to California very soon. With proper food and care, you will not recognize her when she returns." A slight frown creased the unlined forehead. "I feel as if she needs me to do this immediately, but I think it unwise for her to travel alone, and I still have some negotiations to complete here."

She handed a bone-white china cup filled with a delicately scented tea to both men. Her eyes met Balthazar's. "Let me ask you, Lieutenant, why you should find it so hard to believe that the spirits of the dead could communicate with us? The radio telescope here in Arecibo still registers the powerful rumble of the explosion that created our universe many millions of years ago. Scientists can measure that with sensitive instruments. Why then can I not sense her husband's presence? Besides, do you not agree that this would be an excellent way for Emily to receive the care and companionship she desperately needs?"

"I agree that she needs help, and very soon." Balthazar answered evasively.

"Yes, and I will undertake that regardless of whether or not we decide to relocate here. Of course, we must still acquire the country club which adjoins her property. We need more land than she has, although her holdings are extensive. And the country club has the facilities we need. I spoke to the current president, Eduardo Fonseca, this morning. He told me that since so many of their members live near Luquillo and Fajardo, they have long considered relocating further south. It seems Mr. Fonseca himself has some land there that would be ideal for a new club. One of the major stockholders has been opposed in the past, but when I mentioned the price I was considering to Mr. Fonseca, he seemed pleased. He felt that the man's objections could be overcome."

"You've moved very quickly," Balthazar said.

"Yes," Serena replied. "The spirits do not compel, but they do impel. And when you have understood their directions, they smooth all difficulties. At present, I feel some disturbance here. But it will be resolved, I'm sure. Puerto Rico is unquestionably the spirits' choice. Its people have long honored these spirits, although under different forms, starting with the gentle Taino Indians. There seems to be harmony here between man and nature and, especially compared to many of its neighbors, Puerto Rico has had a peaceful history. One could call it an enchanted island."

"Pathologist called from Forensic in San Juan after lunch. Full report on its way, but your corpse's like the others. This one died of marrow cancer. Given bone measurements, a fairly young man. Shot with a .25 caliber. Brief exposure to water." Terron yawned. The late afternoon sun filtered through the open metal shutters on the two windows high up in the wall of the stuffy inner room at the Loiza station. Two electric fans spun back and forth, stirring the dust on the piles of folders and maps on top of the gray filing cabinets.

"And the Voodoo ceremony. Checked it out," Terron rubbed his eyes with the heel of his hand. "Looks like it's going to be up at *El Yunque* late tomorrow afternoon. Somebody called the Catalina Field Office of the Caribbean National Forest and asked if they'd need a permit. They don't. You only need one for camping. Not a large group of them—at most, a couple of buses. No parking problem. Said they'd be around *La Mina* Falls. That's down from the main Visitor's Center. Anyway, that time of day, the tourists' buses are gone."

"Is that area close to the road?" Balthazar asked.

"Pretty close. Couple of small parking lots on your way up through the rain forest. Park in the first one, it's an easy walk down. You sure you want to monitor this?"

"I think so," Balthazar replied resignedly.

"Might find out something." Terron reached over and pulled down a rolled-up map, blew the dust from it and spread it out on the rickety folding table at which they were seated. "Forest ranger says you could have a good vantage point from this observation tower. Looks over the whole area. You couldn't hear much, but we could run over to the Carolina Headquarters, pick up a few of the small mikes. You could spread them around."

Balthazar nodded.

"Car you're using doesn't have a radio. Take one of the jeeps. Good on that road up the mountain anyway."

"By the way," Balthazar said, "we heard a . . . story about Albin—the old knife sharpener—being out on the beach at night a lot. Was he ever interviewed?"

"One of the boys talked to him, but at the time I thought there was no point in writing it up. Albin was having one of his crazier days. Probably could have tried him again later . . . too bad. I sent him to San Juan."

"Why?" Balthazar asked in surprise.

"Well, technically it's required . . . waste of time in this case, of course. Drinking . . . but I'd have thought the donkey was pretty reliable."

"You got him on a drunk charge and sent him to San Juan?"

"No." Now Terron looked surprised. "For the autopsy. Victims of hit-and-runs. Supposed to do it."

"He's dead?"

"Late last night. Whoever hit him caught the donkey broadside and poor Albin landed some distance away. One of our patrols saw the donkey lying by the road and knew right away what had happened. Car going pretty fast, comes around the curve. The donkey must have been in the middle of the road and Albin

154 M. J. ADAMSON

more or less asleep on his back. Trees on both sides of the road along there. Pretty dark."

"You're sure it was an accident?"

"Only way I'd think it wasn't would be if the autopsy shows no alcohol in his system. That's unlikely. Old guy'd go on a binge every couple months. He was about due, I figure. Bound to happen one of these days. He never had just a couple of drinks when he started."

"Suppose somebody gave him a bottle, sent him off, and then ran him down?"

"What for?" Terron tried to conceal his impatience. "Suppose Albin had seen something on the beach night before last. He wouldn't tell us, and if he mentioned it to anyone else, they wouldn't pay attention. Sometimes Albin would say rational-type things, but then next sentence he'd start telling you how he'd met Jesus walking on the road. Like I say, too bad, but . . . to get back to the Voodoo thing. Heard the Haitians are here."

"Plural?"

"The head man and three drummers. Have to have them come, too. Can't believe anybody around here's been practicing on those drums. One of the drummers apparently speaks Spanish. He can translate, I guess, if the spirit that's speaking through the head man doesn't happen to know it." He snorted and shook his head in irritated wonder.

20

ON ITS WAY to the rain forest, Highway 191 cuts through the narrow streets of a small town called both Mameyes and Palmer, and goes past sunny lowlands with grazing cattle and a slow, transparent river. Then it begins a steep, winding climb. With each half mile, the light slowly diminishes as the canopy of foliage thickens, and the temperature drops another degree. The smell of wet, rich earth intensifies and everywhere moisture shines on glossy green leaves. One begins to feel that the smell is of the color green.

It was only a little after nine in the morning, and Balthazar and Sixto saw no oncoming cars. In any case according to Terron, the highway had been blocked at the top by a landslide for a very long time. Even the signs advising the driver of that fact had rusted. But one hairpin curve followed another and the road was just two cars wide. Sixto concentrated on his driving, pleased at the police jeep's response.

But it was not, they had already agreed, going to be easy to find a place—outside of a parking lot—to leave the car where the jeep's distinctive blue and white markings would not be immediately visible. On one side of the road the mountain slopes, covered with tall trees and drooping vines, rose wall-like to the sky. On the other side, the drop was almost vertical. There were few turnoffs.

They intended to get set up well before the crowd arrived in the early afternoon. They needed to plant a few small microphones in what they hoped were strategic positions and get into place themselves in the observation tower that overlooked the falls. The Forest Service had agreed to put a Closed For Repairs sign on its door.

When they finally arrived at the top of the round medieval tower, Sixto, scanning the area through his binoculars, announced that the view was perfect. Whether he was commenting on its beauty or its usefulness in terms of observation, Balthazar couldn't decide. He himself was still sitting on the top step of the spiral staircase, trying to catch his breath. Being a detective in the country clearly required stamina.

The patrolman who had delivered the microphones from Carolina just before they left that morning had asked with a smirk if they planned on bugging trees and rocks. That was just what they had done—slithering down trails full of wet leaves, scrambling over the boulders. Balthazar rubbed his aching knee and thought nostalgically of the sidewalks of New York. Nice, level concrete slabs, with delicatessens on the corners.

He took a sip of the coffee from the thermos, and a bite of a sandwich from the backpack. He chewed slowly, and then lifted up a corner of the bread, peering at the white juicy meat inside. "This is delicious" he said.

"Roast pig," Sixto replied. "Terron says Panama gets it from that open-air stand next to the cemetery. Oh, and we must remember to go there."

"Probably right. Terron says none of those graves have been disturbed, but—"

"No, the pig-roasting place. That's why my mother called. Cousin Ida's neighbor says the old men there use mango wood to cook the pig and that's what gives it such good taste. Mama wants three pounds, not too much fat."

Balthazar got up, savoring the last of the sandwich. While Puerto Rico had wonderful pastrami, he reflected, you couldn't get pig slowly roasted over mango wood in Manhattan. Besides, the sidewalks would be icy now.

He walked to the nearest slit-like opening and took out his own binoculars. The streams of white water first snaked, then cascaded down the dark stones, collecting in a clear pool at the bottom and then spilling down huge moss-covered slabs of rocks as far down as one could see. Terron had been right. The tower was an ideal vantage point.. The falls between two sharply rising slopes formed a natural amphitheater, just waiting for the actors to arrive. Near the pool at the bottom were four stone picnic pavilions with tiled roofs.

He put the plastic receiver in his ear and almost jumped. Around them the quiet of the forest was noisy with the sounds of a million tiny tree frogs, insects, and birds, but as he switched from one microphone to another, he picked up an individual call so close that he felt the bird was on his shoulder.

In the far distance, beyond the mist and gray light of the rain forest, he could see the sun shining on Luquillo Beach, and on the tall buildings of the shimmering condominiums that ringed a further shore. If the wait was going to be long, at least one wasn't shivering and staring at a grimy warehouse.

But the preparations for the ceremony began much earlier than the two men had expected. The first group to arrive were all young people in their teens. They hurried exuberantly down the path carrying boxes, plastic supermarket bags, huge iron pots, and several crates of wildly complaining chickens. All were dressed in white, obviously preparing for a party. They dumped their bundles on the stone picnic tables and chased each other nimbly back up the steep path, dodging the older women coming down more slowly. They too were dressed in white, from their kerchiefs to their shoes, and they had their arms full.

A familiar soprano voice floated up to the tower. Lorena Garcia was laughing but her tone was the purposeful one of a general deploying troops. They must have appeased her by putting her in charge of the arrangements, Balthazar thought. Not only did she have the voice for it, she obviously had a flair for command. With great efficiency, she promptly put some of the boys in charge of building fires in the brick enclosures in the huts, while others filled the huge pots with water from the stream. Others, when they were not chasing the girls, selected several small areas to be cleared with their machetes. On some open spots, they neatly stacked the armloads of dry driftwood they'd carried down.

Some of the girls were scampering around placing hundreds of white candles near the pool and around the pavilions. Others were helping the women with the food preparation, opening up large bags of rice, pouring bowls of beans into boiling water. Balthazar was surprised to see that the young so greatly outnumbered the old, but, despite their boisterous horseplay, they were clearly useful.

Several of the older women were busy setting up an altar on a pavilion table. It was carefully covered with white pillowcases and then various items were, after intense discussion, scattered around. As the microphone picked up a vigorous argument about the proper way to please the spirits in setting out the opened cans of tuna fish, painted gourds and coconut bowls, Balthazar considered the wonderful uses of modern technology. Lorena herself took charge of one end of the altar, endlessly rearranging some black candles and a heavy wooden black cross. On its arms she put two stacks of the large cards used by Tarot readers. The placement of some bottles and pitchers occupied her for some time because she found it necessary to stop repeatedly and scrutinize the total effect.

Finally, slowly and with enormous dignity, Junior Pabon descended the narrow path. His white shirt was open to the waist, and Balthazar nudged Sixto and pointed to the old man's chest. Several strands of bright-colored polished stones, as well as a black rosary, and what looked like a Star of David on another thin chain decorated it. In one hand Junior carried a long black silk scarf and in the other a carved wooden statue—a representation of Loiza's favorite saint, the Apostle James the Elder, dressed as a warrior, with his sword aloft. He placed these things on the altar, and then paced around the edge of the picnic area, peering closely at the cleared patches. Finally satisfied with one, he took a stick and began drawing serpentine squiggles in the soft earth.

Three black men in broad-brimmed hats had followed him down the path, each carrying a large drum resembling an upside-down cone with the point cut off. All of the instruments were brightly painted and obviously new. The men positioned themselves near the altar and began tapping the drums tentatively, their eyes fixed on one another, as if they were trying to see the rhythm as well as hear it. One lighter-skinned man took off his hat and wiped his forehead. Balthazar straightened. The man looked familiar. He wondered, not for the first time, if people of one race always had trouble distinguishing those of another unless they were well acquainted. The cadence of the drumbeats, although still hesitant, was becoming pronounced. It sounded oddly modern, like jazz syncopation.

Junior Pabon continued his earth drawing, occasionally glancing up at the drummers, sometimes checking with Lorena. She was truly enjoying herself, but Pabon looked worried. Balthazar wondered why the Haitian *hougan* hadn't appeared. Perhaps there was some sort of ritual he had to perform first. Or perhaps it was a way of keeping the audience in suspense, anticipating the entrance of the star performer.

Abruptly Pabon clapped his hands and motioned one of the young men to bring over a crate of white chickens. Immediately everyone stopped work and hurried to crowd around. After due consideration, Pabon selected a chicken, and holding it under one skinny arm, threw a handful of grain over the drawing he had made in the dirt. The chicken, excited by the crowd and the noise, fluttered and squawked, but when it was put on the ground, it showed some interest in the grain. That excited the crowd, and some of the boys loudly urged the chicken to eat. It grabbed a kernel, and shouts of approval filled the air. Lorena scooped up the struggling chicken and, strutting with self-importance, carried it through the crowd, making sure she brushed everyone with its wings or body.

When she handed it back to Pabon, he lifted the chicken above his head and pointed it in all four directions. The drums accelerated wildly. Then he lowered it and quickly and expertly wrung its neck.

Bright blood spurted out, and, lifting the dead bird, he let the blood run down his face.

Many of the girls jumped back, some screaming, some with high nervous giggles. Pabon offered the chicken's limp body to Lorena. She clearly wasn't eager, but she let some of the blood dribble down her chin and onto her dress. Several of the older women followed suit. The last woman carried the carcass to a table and began plucking the feathers.

The sacrifice was repeated several times. If a chicken refused to eat, it was returned reluctantly to the crate and another was selected. Some of the boys grew bolder, and chased the girls around the falls with the still fluttering, but headless fowls. The girls sometimes allowed themselves to be brushed, sometimes ran among the rocks, falling into the pool, helpless with laughter. By contrast, the few older people went through the rites unsmilingly.

It was well past four. Already the light in the rain forest was starting to fade. The bonfires were lit. Balthazar lowered his binoculars and looked at Sixto. "There are a couple of things really wrong here," he said in a troubled voice.

"Perhaps, but I've never been to a Voodoo ceremony before."

"No, I meant . . . well, look around. I think the Haitian guy should be killing those chickens, not Junior Pabon. And where is Momée Molina?"

"*Sí.*" I do not see Ana anywhere, either. Her grandmother would find it difficult to keep her away."

"That's another thing, where the hell are all the older people? And Lorena Garcia said she kept the drums, but those look new. And I swear we've seen that end drummer before."

Sixto turned his binoculars on the man's face, studied it, and then snapped his fingers in irritation. "The waiter at the Restaurante!"

"God, you're right. I should have recognized him."

Balthazar began hastily stuffing their equipment in the backpack. "This performance is for *our* benefit. The real one is somewhere else. And I bet it's down in Loiza Aldea."

Sixto was already clattering down the metal stairs. "Wait by the road. I will bring the jeep," he called back over his shoulder.

Balthazar stood slightly back from the roadside next to a bush that was dripping icily on his shoulder. The disappearing sun had only lightly touched the tops of the tallest trees all day. That, and the altitude, made him shiver in his light shirt. His thoughts made him even more uncomfortable. He strained to hear the jeep's motor over the pounding of the drums.

How long had Sixto been gone—five minutes, ten? Had the elder townspeople become so anxious that they, possibly along with some of the younger men, guarded the jeep, waiting to intercept the detectives? Were they waiting in ambush somewhere, expecting him to check on Sixto's whereabouts? He slipped out his gun.

Still, a direct confrontation seemed unlikely. Why was it so necessary that he and Sixto be kept away from the Voodoo ceremony? Or was it *any* outsider the old people wanted to exclude?

Probably Sixto had taken the time to raise Terron on the radio. If the Sergeant could get to the real ceremony in time, he could at least report what was said, what was done. Up until now, no one had worried about what the local men might discover.

One thing was different, now. Serena's arrival had meant land would be changing hands. But the land had always been for sale. No one denied that. Most of the poor wanted to live nearer neighbors in town, and the middle-class were anxious for the status of the mountain locations.

The land was reasonably priced. Residents and

newcomers agreed. Everybody who might conceivably want the land seemed to have money, or be able to raise it. Victor Malen and his partner, good old joking Fred McMurdie, had business expertise and, given their businesses in Haiti, would know something about Voodoo, but they could have bought half the island. Josh Sterling, with or without Serena's financial backing, could easily have put partnerships together. The corporations that owned some of the larger plots might have wanted in on an assemblage deal, but, if not, would hardly be frightened away by dead bodies left on the beach. Neither would Emily deDiego, who lived in her own private world, surrounded by her own dead. And, although she had said she didn't want to sell, no one had bothered to find out whether she meant it by making a cash offer.

Balthazar impatiently checked his watch. That was useless—he didn't know when Sixto had left the tower. In any case, it would take him some time to explain to Terron, find out what the Sergeant knew.

Smuggling? Drug smugglers had enough money to corrupt the little carved wooden statues of saints, let alone mortal men. After a few runs, they could have bought any acreage that bordered the beach.

The two mayors probably didn't personally have a lot of money. Yet Montanez seemed a reasonable man and, given his influence, should have been able to cut himself in on any deal going. Wouldn't a mayor have something to do with rezoning?

Loiza's mayor, Couvertier, was crazy enough to have some fixation about a transformed town, bustling with rich tourists. Certainly his elaborate beachfront project, built no doubt with city money, indicated that. But why go through intricate machinations to frighten the people away when most would gladly sell? Could he not even have the land condemned, forcibly sold? What idea of his would ruin Terron and Panama's plan, whatever that was?

Why would anyone want to frighten those people? And where the hell was Sixto?

He stepped quickly out into the road, deciding

edgily that he'd walk up just far enough to see around the curve. No doubt Sixto would leave the lights off until they were further. . . .

The school bus, its headlights off, hurtled around the curve, heading in a nightmare flash straight toward him. Balthazar scrambled back into the bushes, trying desperately to steady his two hands on the gun. The bus, its open door flapping, screeched to a stop.

Sixto grinned down at him from the driver's seat.

He pulled himself up the two steps by the handrail and the bus shot forward, bouncing him painfully into the aisle. "You have to sit down," Sixto yelled cheerfully. "I do not know how to operate the door yet."

Balthazar fell, rather than sat, into the seat directly behind the driver's as Sixto took the next curve directly in the middle of the road. "Do not worry," he assured Balthazar. "It's much faster to take this down the middle. But I'll be able to see the lights of a driver coming up."

"What's the matter with the jeep?" Balthazar leaped over, his mouth next to Sixto's ear. Not only was the bus's motor deafening, its brakes squealed at the slightest touch and the folding door slammed open at every turn.

"*Two* flat tires," Sixto said firmly. "And the radio disconnected. I am sorry about the bus. There were nice vans in the parking lot. But they might have had burglar alarms. And this door was easy to force with my key chain sword. Bent it, though."

Balthazar looked at the ignition. "Where are the keys?"

Sixto wrenched the big wheel as the bus skittered toward the sheer drop on the road. The clumsy vehicle rocked, but miraculously rounded the next corner still upright.

"There were no keys," Sixto shouted, laughing. "But there was aluminum foil in the trash can. Growing up in San Juan you do not learn to ride a horse. But you learn other things." He was enjoying himself enormously.

"Brakes okay on this thing?"

"*Sí.* I think. But the tires—they have hardly any tread."

Balthazar leaned back and closed his eyes.

The pay phone in the bar in Mameyes, a.k.a. Palmer, was right next to the jukebox. Balthazar was shouting at Terron, but he could at least hear him clearly.

"Been worried, tried to raise you on the radio for the last two hours," Terron was saying. "Especially after I heard that Panama's cook didn't take the afternoon off."

Balthazar put his finger in the ear nearest the jukebox. "What? Did you say Panama's *cook* . . . ?"

"Right. Knew we were on the wrong track."

"How?" Balthazar glared at the slim young man pumping quarters in the machine and pounding the plastic top in time to the salsa beat. The young man grinned back, unabashed.

"Her cook's been working all day in the kitchen, using Panama's big pots to make a lot of food for the ceremony. But Panama said it was funny because the waiter left early. And the cook stayed. So did the food. So I started checking right away. Think I know where they really are."

"Where?" Balthazar screamed.

"At the mayor's project, down on the beach. Velez can show you the fastest way there. I'll have him meet you where Highway 3 turns off into Rio Grande. Got an idea how to get you there without much notice. Velez'll be driving a city repair van."

"Okay," Balthazar shouted. "We're in a school bus." He hung up hurriedly. Climbing back into the bus, he found he was even recalling the muggers in Central Park with some nostalgia.

21

BARRELING DOWN the dark, curvy, two-lane road, Velez was talking as fast as he was driving. The shocks on the city's enclosed van were, if anything, worse than those on the bus. Perched on a shifting pile of boards behind the driver's seat, jostled from side to side, Balthazar and Sixto strained to catch the details of Terron's plan.

". . . boat yard with a chain link fence next to the restaurant. The restaurant is open-air on three sides, just has grillwork that you can slide back. Stage for the musicians in the back. There's a little office in the boat yard that overlooks the beach and you can get up on its roof and look right down into the restaurant and the bandstand. The roof's flat. . . ."

He swerved sharply. "Sorry . . . almost hit that dog." Balthazar and Sixto clambered back up on the boards, which had skidded out from under them. Sixto rubbed the elbow on which he had landed, but grinned cheerfully. "As I was saying, you can get up on the roof from a metal ladder built onto the side of the building. Then around the roof there's a couple rows of concrete blocks where you can get down. . . ."

But by that time they were nearing the beach and Velez's voice was lost in the pounding rise and fall of the drums. Amplified by loudspeakers on the stage, the incessant beat seemed to engulf them, tuning the phrasing of their thoughts to the rapid rhythm. Velez's last words, "YOU CAN GET DOWN, YOU CAN GET

DOWN," echoed in Balthazar's head, their inflection dictated by the drums' seductive beat. It was not difficult to imagine a trance being induced by their insistency.

"Not bad, eh?" Velez roared. "Catchy beat. They were playing *merengue* music earlier, foolishly trying to throw us off." He wriggled the van through the closely parked cars and pulled up behind the fenced concrete block building. He took out a key, pointed to the padlock and then backed up the road a considerable distance to indicate where he would be parked. Handing Balthazar a small walkie-talkie, he shrugged with a smile as he did so, waving in the direction of the drums. They clambered out of the van and opened the padlocked gate.

Clutching the narrow rungs of the ladder on the boathouse wall, Sixto climbed lightly upwards. Balthazar followed more slowly, trying to keep his knee straight, fumbling in the dark for the next metal step. His breath rasped in his throat. As he reached the roof, he could just make out Sixto, scuttling crab-wise to the low railing overlooking the lighted restaurant. Grimacing, stooping as low as he could, Balthazar hobbled across the graveled roof and squatted beside him. They were directly in the path of one of the loudspeakers. The drums could almost be felt as well as heard.

The scene below was partly lit by the three-quarter moon, partly by the flicker of bonfires on the beach. Most of the crowd was jammed into the small restaurant or on the concrete apron outside where the young usually danced to quite different music. But these people were almost all gray-haired, almost all wore white, and all were staring with solemn intensity up at the dimly-lit stage. From their unmoving silence, their fixed gazes, Balthazar could see they were not expecting a drama, a representation of reality, but reality itself.

A few pale yellow spotlights focused on the Watusi-tall, gaunt black man with an oiled, shaven head who stood in the center of the stage wearing only an immaculate white cloth that hung from his waist to his knees. Every sharp bone in his skeletal upper body protruded.

Swaying with his eyes closed, he clasped the collar of a small white goat with lighted candles tied to its horns. The goat's eyes rolled, its mouth hung open, but its bleat could not be heard above the drums. Feet planted wide apart before a thin, painted pillar, one undulating matchstick arm flung out, the man seemed unaware of the panicked goat's cries, unconscious of his own surroundings. On a platform atop the pillar, a thick snake lay coiled. Motionless, it held its narrow head erect. Its lidless eyes and the intricate markings on its head and body glittered in the spotlight trained on it. Deep in the shadows, only the disembodied hands of the drummers, blurred with the speed of their movement, were visible.

The ornamental concrete blocks that Balthazar and Sixto crouched behind had patterned openings. Looking through these, Balthazar turned his binoculars on the people below. A flick of the *hougan*'s wrist, and the drummers slowed the beat a hypnotic half second. As if compelled by that cadence, the audience began to sway in unison, but their blank, unsmiling faces reflected no pleasure in their robotic motions.

Sixto jabbed his elbow in Balthazar's ribs and gestured toward the fringes of the crowd. Standing on a pile of boulders on the beach itself were Serena and the two Sterlings. From a slightly higher vantage point, Josh loomed behind the two women, who wore long white robes. Their stillness was so perfect they seemed a group carved by an eclectic sculptor who had chosen from an assortment of pagan deities. This impression was heightened when they were caught by the occasional flare of the bonfires as one of the young men tending them threw on a splash of gasoline and, undoubtedly, given the heavy lingering aroma, a handful of incense and herbs.

Suddenly, one of the drummers barked a command, and Momée Molina appeared, moving with ponderous grace through the transfixed audience to the stage. She grasped the goat's collar and leaned over it, caressing it everywhere, murmuring to it, soothing it.

The wave of drum beats lessened slightly, as she offered the goat some grain stalks, coaxing it to eat. It sniffed at her hand and then nibbled at the food, darting troubled glances around the stage. She lifted a triumphant arm to the crowd. They shouted back at her. She circled among them, leading the goat, and everyone pushed and shoved to touch it, to rub against it.

As she returned to the stage, the drums hammered furiously. Standing next to the *hougan*, she lifted the goat's front legs up and put them on her shoulders. She pressed against the goat; because of her white dress and the faint light, their bodies seemed to merge. Then, still holding tightly to the goat's front legs, she twisted her body abruptly to the right.

The *hougan* lifted a sharp, thin knife up to the snake, as if to salute it, and then swooping down, with one quick stroke, severed the goat's testicles. Blood ran down the thin, white legs and over the hooves. Its one high bleat shrilled even above the drums.

Swiftly, the *hougan* moved behind the goat, pushing it down onto its four legs, then pinioning its body between his knees. Again he whirled the gleaming blade high, leaned forward over the animal, and sliced open its throat. Its head slumped forward, but he controlled its convulsions with his own legs. A bowl held beneath caught the frothing blood.

He released the goat's body and, holding the bowl almost imploringly up to the motionless reptile, took several small sips. He began a high-pitched incomprehensible chant.

Blindly, he thrust the bowl at the woman and staggered forward to the edge of the stage, his head bent. The crowd surged closer. The drums now drowned out every sound. The *hougan* threw back his head, his chin wet with blood and saliva, his eyes rolled back until only the whites showed. He raised his thin arms slowly and stretching them out, put his palms together, and began to weave them and his body in a snake-like motion. Even his bones seemed to melt.

Momée raised the bowl to the pillar. The snake flicked its tongue lasciviously. "Damballah!" she shrieked. The drums, too, said *DAMBALLAH* again and again. Balthazar found he could not think anything except that single incantation. Slowly, majestically, the snake bent his head slightly over the edge of the platform.

DAMBALLAH, the drums chanted, without losing rhythm, but seeming to grow muted. The *hougan* began to speak, his words sibilant, his voice low but picked up by the microphone. His hissing noises resolved themselves into syllables, and then into Spanish words. Some of the people cried out in amazement, but they were quickly stilled by the others.

"I am Damballah, I am Damballah. *Loa* of the river, of the waters." The *hougan*'s tongue darted out from between his lips. "I speak for the sea. For the sea, for my brother, *Agwé-taroyo*, *loa* of the sea. We have come to warn, to warn our followers. To warn them of the wind. Listen, listen, listen."

The drums softly but insistently, repeated that word now: *LISTEN, LISTEN.* Again the man's tongue flicked. "Soon, soon, September. Waves will come, waves higher than houses, waves that will wash walls away, take away the sand, the earth. Leave, leave, leave. There is no safety by the water. I, Damballah tell you so. I, Damballah."

The man's body swayed without ceasing; the words seemed to come from another mouth than his. Above him, the snake twisted its blunt-nosed head from side to side, in time with the words, in tune with the drums.

Balthazar put down his binoculars and looked at Sixto, still staring intently through his at the stage. A hurricane, he thought, but the drums only let him think that one word. He shut his eyes and put his fingers in his ears, trying to wrench his mind from the maddening, repetitious pattern. A hurricane. . . . Hadn't Terron mentioned there had been one some thirty years earlier? These old people would remember it vividly, recall how dangerous it was, remember the death it had left in its destructive wake.

That was the message then, a long-range weather forecast. Leave. They should abandon their land.

In a frantic effort to concentrate, he summoned up Terron's face as he had first seen him in the restaurant, the morning after they had arrived. Terron had talked of the hurricane and he had said ". . . people moved out there a long time ago because it was unused." That was the point. The land was unused, so they just built on it. But it probably wasn't *their* land.

But wait, he thought, frantically trying to piece together what he knew: now they had a claim; it would be their land, at least in a way. They had built there, even fenced in portions for their animals, lived there for thirty years. They were squatters, and squatters had rights. The original owners would have to take that into account. They could not sell easily.

The old people were squatters with children in Boston and New York, some of them educated, all of whom believed this *was* their parents' land, their grand-parents' land. Court cases for years. Even if the buyer would pay the squatters and the owners enough, some would not settle, some would be like Emily deDiego. Some old people would not want to leave their land. The legal squabble would be eternal.

What had Felicity Sterling said about Emily deDiego's land?—"her title was not clouded." Her husband had told her that. Was Josh Sterling then also thinking about squatters' rights? If you had Emily deDiego's land, as Serena intended, and the country club, you would already be a giant's step forward toward a large assemblage of beach front. But Serena had said someone with shares did not want to sell the country club land. In any case, before this week Serena hadn't seemed to know about Emily, and could not have been sure her approach would work. . . .

He turned his binoculars quickly on the Sterlings. Josh was holding tightly to his wife's arm and seemed to be frantically shouting in her ear. She was struggling to shake off his grasp and still keep her own footing on the rocks. As Balthazar watched, she wrenched her arm free, jumped down on the sand, and began moving rapidly toward the restaurant. As she strode by a fire's glare, the light flickered over the anger in her face. Serena, moving almost trance-like, followed her.

Balthazar shook Sixto's arm and pointed down to one of the overturned wooden boats next to the fence, then again moved crab-wise swiftly to the ladder and scrambled down. Sixto was behind him, but reached the top of the boat first. From there, they could see directly into the restaurant. Felicity was firmly making her way through the still swaying crowd.

The *hougan's* voice continued hypnotically repeating his message, warning of the danger ahead. The people's eyes were on him and on the snake, now draped partly over the platform's edge, looking as if it were contemplating slithering down the pole. No one moved to stop Felicity. With her elegant head held high, her purposeful walk, her loose robe, she looked as if she were part of the ceremony.

She mounted the side stairs of the stage and faced the drummers. Then she raised her foot and kicked hard at each of the narrow bases of the drums. All three instruments went sprawling. One rolled over and over off the stage. One surprised drummer was still beating his hands against the empty air. The din ceased abruptly.

Whirling toward the people, she screamed, "No!" Her voice echoed in the absolute silence. She gazed fiercely down at the sea of shocked faces. "Damballah is not here. Damballah *es no aqui*!" This is not a true ceremony!" She paused, whether to control her anger or to recall her Spanish, Balthazar couldn't determine.

Then in the silence, he heard the thud of horse's hooves in the sand. Heads turned toward the sound. Those on the far edges began shrieking, "Saint James! Saint James. He comes! Another miracle!"

In the moonlight, a white horse was running wildly, the figure on its back indistinct. But there was an upright stick in the rider's hand, looking much like a raised sword. The horse plunged toward the tightly-packed crowd without slowing, and people leapt, scrambling madly out of its way. The rider slid off on the edge of the apron, but the horse ran forward still. A young fire-tender lunged at the animal, grabbing its mane. Half guiding the frenzied beast, half yanked by it, he hung on until it almost slammed against the fence near where Balthazar and Sixto were balancing on top of the over-turned boat. The horse reared, but the young man clung grimly to the mane and at last the horse stopped, quivering and dancing.

In the meantime, the crowd, first bent on getting out of the way of the horse's flailing hooves, was now just as frantically avoiding the man. There were a few cries of "A *zombi!*" But most drew back in horrified silence. The newcomer lurched forward beneath the sickly yellow spotlights onto the wooden floor of the restaurant, supporting himself with his stick. Balthazar himself could do nothing but stare. The man had only half a face.

The side Balthazar could see was caked with thick, dried blood which had come from a puckered, ugly hole in the temple, and from the socket that once held an eye. A bullet had smashed out through the cheekbone, caving in that side of the face. The man turned his head blindly, trying to focus his remaining eye, and with a chill Balthazar recognized Manuel, Emily deDiego's caretaker. The injured man saw the *hougan* and raised one trembling arm, pointing at the *hougan* and opening his mouth, but the only sound that came out was a hoarse rattle. Desperately, he tried again.

"*Mal* . . ." he stammered, the Spanish word for evil.

In the horrified silence, Manuel staggered toward the stage. Seeing Serena standing before him, he moved toward her with an odd, beseeching gesture, his lips moving, his free arm outstretched, clawing the space that separated him from her. He reached Serena, and began again, this time waving his arm in the direction of the deDiego land. "La Señora . . . ," he cried wildly, urgently pointing back toward the direction from which he'd come. Unable to finish the sentence, he fell forward against her. A huge gout of red blood spilled from his lips, staining her white robe.

Manuel was not a large man, and she was not only a tall woman, but a strong one. Nevertheless, his collapse shoved her back against the stage. Because of its support, she did not fall, but she could not hold the man's dead weight. He slid down and lay, crumpled, at her feet. She bent over him, then knelt beside him and put his damaged head in her lap, crooning words of incomprehensible consolation.

No one moved. Dull-eyed, the *hougan* stood, his arms now at his side, like an actor having difficulty coming out of his role. Felicity Sterling was at his side, but her eyes were on Serena and Manuel below her.

"Lieutenant, Lieutenant!" Josh Sterling's face was contorted with urgency. "Damn, damn," he clung to the posts of the fence, obviously having great difficulty in speaking. "I shouldn't have told Felicity now, knowing how she feels about using Voodoo to harm. . . . But when I heard him say those people should move, I knew. I knew the reason for the bodies. Without thinking, I blurted it out. The squatters. How hard it would be to get rid of these people legally. The law says if they've been occupying the land openly and hostilely for a certain amount of years, then they . . . If I'd been seriously looking at land here, I would have caught it months ago. But it wasn't until Serena got interested, that I got the maps, that I started. . . . And I had to hide them from Felicity or she'd worry that I myself was getting interested. . . . You see what I'm saying? You understand? This land could be very valuable, maybe, if you had a big assemblage, but you'd have a real problem—"

"Yes, yes, that's what I think now, too. But do you know who already has enough? Whose the most likely—?"

Josh shrugged impatiently. "Matter of record, maybe. But there's a group of corporations . . . if they're privately held, a list of stockholders would be difficult. . . . Look, I've got to go up there and grab Felicity. She's so mad, she's likely to scratch that hougan guy's—"

"We need him." Balthazar snapped, eying Sterling's powerful build. "But the deDiego woman may be hurt. I've got to—"

"I'll sit on the son of a bitch if necessary." Josh shoved forward, almost lifting people bodily out of his way.

Sixto was standing with one foot on the boat and one on top of the fence. "The old woman. The caretaker came for help? She is hurt, you think? Perhaps she is bleeding to death?"

Balthazar was frantically slapping his pockets. "I must have dropped the damned walkie . . . climbing down. Maybe it's at the bottom of the ladder, or—"

"The beach," Sixto cut in. "Faster than the road, even. Straight line. A mile maybe? I could run. . . ." He stopped and looked down at the horse right below him, still being held precariously by the young man.

"Best way," Sixto said decisively, but with real trepidation in his voice. "Get back," he yelled at the startled teenager and leaped forward, almost belly-flopping on top of the horse. The frightened mare threw her front hooves high in the air but came down running. Sixto seemed to be clinging to the animal with every part of his body: fingers, wrists, elbows, thighs, knees. But miraculously he stayed on. The frenzied horse galloped down the beach toward the deDiego estate.

Velez came running around the side of the concrete boat-yard office. "I heard the drums stop. Just like that," he panted. "Thought I'd better come in a hurry. Jeep's outside. Any trouble?"

"Okay, okay." Balthazar moved forward toward the gate, hanging on to Velez's arm. "You get on that stage. I want that witch doctor or whatever he is held. I don't care *what* he tells you—he does speak Spanish. Find out what he knows. I told Sterling—the big bald guy—to grab him. He can fill you in. There's a badly injured man there. I'll get on the radio, send an ambulance over and some help for you. Need an ambulance out at the deDiego place, too. I'll take the jeep. Sixto's on his way there."

"How did he—?" Velez began.

But Balthazar was already climbing into the jeep, reaching for the radio.

22

Sixto suddenly realized that he had forgotten to breathe, so concentrated were his efforts to stay mounted. He wound his fingers tighter in the thick mane and let out his breath. After its first panicked spurt, the horse had settled into a gallop, but Sixto decided he was at least on the edge of gaining control. The mare was running on the well-packed sand near the edge of the water. Its hooves hit the surface firmly and rhythmically.

He looked between its ears. The bright moonlight outlined jagged rocks and driftwood logs. The horse no doubt would be able to avoid them, he assured himself. He'd once heard horses were stupid animals, but surely, he decided, they themselves would want to avoid falling. If the animal stumbled, would he be pitched forward over its head, or would she roll on her side on top of him? Perhaps if he weren't hanging on so firmly, he might be thrown clear. But his fingers insisted on their anxious grip.

Ahead he could see the tops of the tall pines surrounding the deDiego house. When they swayed in the wind, he could even make out the broken ruins of the third story.

If he could slow the horse now so that it would be walking quietly, perhaps he could slip unnoticed through the grounds to the house. His instinct told him that Emily deDiego was in immense danger. Manuel might have wounded whoever attacked him—the man might still be there, and might still be armed. Unless, he thought, the old woman, crazy with fear, had herself mistakenly shot the caretaker. She would be no less dangerous. But if he called to her, it would alert anyone else, and even if he yelled "Police," she might not believe him.

Yet if she had wounded him, why did Manuel accuse the *hougan*? Evil, he had called the man. Was his ragged cry an accusation? Riding frantically for help toward those drums with the fierce agony throbbing in his head must certainly have confused the badly injured man.

The little river that bordered the deDiego property glinted just ahead in the moonlight. Sixto yanked on the mane. The horse jerked its head up, but did not slow. Perversely, it began to run faster.

Somehow, he would have to slide off the animal's back. Just after crossing the river. That was the best plan. Try for the soft sand. The horse would keep running, and anyone seeing it riderless in the moonlight would think it returning home of its own accord. The water would doubtless slow its mad flight and he could. . . . The mare splashed through the shallow water without missing a stride.

He had to get off. *Now*, thought Sixto, loosening his grip on the mane. Abruptly, unexpectedly, the horse reared upright, neighing frantically. Sixto spun off, landing with a thump on his back, his head bouncing hard on the packed sand.

He lay motionless, feeling the nausea that accompanies the desperate breathlessness of such a fall, then the shocking sensation of collapsing lungs. He thought only of the need for air. After long moments, he struggled up to a sitting position, gasping, blinking, moving his aching head very carefully. Had he blacked out? No. Surely that dull pounding he heard was the horse running a short way in the distance. Or had they started the drums again? Or was the noise in his head? How badly was he hurt?

He leaned on one hand and attempted to get his feet under him, but instead he pitched onto his knees. Dizziness made him retch dryly. On all fours, he bent his head forward. That helped. He touched the back of his skull gingerly. There was a very large lump. That sand had felt like concrete, and given all the rubble that surrounded the house, he might actually have landed on a piece, at that. His ears rang. Perhaps he should crawl to that tree, raise himself up on its trunk.

Inching forward, he put out a hand and touched, not soft sand, but someone's outstretched hand. It was quite cold. Lying in the deep shadows cast by the tree was a body. If the horse had not reared, it would have trampled it. Sixto jerked his own hand back instinctively, then, sucking in his breath, pain and fear churning in his stomach, reached out again and fumbled for the wrist. He could not find a pulse and there was no mistaking that unnatural coldness.

Blearily, he struggled to focus his eyes. He had no flashlight, no matches. His unwilling hand began to search for the head, feeling for the hair. He touched the icy cheek and then the forehead. The blood clotted on the temple was sticky; his fingers came away wet. He swallowed hard. As soon as he touched the hair, he knew, but he groped, and felt the untidy bun at the back of the head. He was too late, then, to save Emily deDiego. He wiped his hand almost unthinkingly on the sand, crawled a little way off, and vomited.

Get to the tree, he thought, but after one more painful effort, he gave up and stretched out limply on the sand. If he blundered through the grounds in the dark, he would be likely to destroy evidence. Not to mention that he himself would be an easy target, should the killer still be there. *Baltasar* would be here soon with men, with lights. It was best to just stay where he was. When he heard the sirens, he could get up and direct them to the body. But right now a tight band of pain radiated out from the base of his skull and circled his forehead, and he could still hear, like an echo of the drums, an uneven thud, which reverberated hollowly. Then two clouds of blackness came around his skull, met on the bridge of his nose, and he stopped thinking. Sixto pressed his cheek against the coolness of the sand and fainted.

The gunshot aroused him. Someone was shouting his name. He jumped to his feet without thinking, reeled, staggered to the tree, and called back. He was still standing, if unsteady, when Balthazar rushed around the corner of the fence and onto the beach.

"I just shot the padlock off the fence. Why didn't you hear me calling?"

When he heard Sixto's abbreviated and somewhat sheepish account, Balthazar directed his flashlight just to the side of his colleague's face. Sixto looked ill, absolutely colorless. Balthazar thought with some relief of the ambulance and medical examiner that would eventually arrive. A concussion could be dangerous and Sixto surely ought. . . .

"We need to check this out now," Sixto insisted, as if reading his thoughts. "There could be someone else here. I thought I heard this . . . noise, this pounding. . . ."

"A blow to the head—"

Sixto interrupted stubbornly. "The equipment and lights will have to come from Carolina. Terron will be busy at the pavilion. It will take them much time. Is there another flashlight?"

In the flashlight's beam, the crumpled body looked even frailer in death than it had in life. Emily deDiego's outflung arm seemed to be making a mute appeal. But whoever had shot her had ignored it, casually taking a palm frond and sweeping away his footprints in the sand. They followed the branch's patterns to the edge of her property. Even if they'd had more light, a trail would have been hard to follow. There was a tangle of dead leaves, and the tough creepers that hugged the ground sprang back immediately. The gentle but persistent east wind was already erasing their own impressions in the loose sandy topsoil.

They swung their flashlights in arcs around the grounds. The tree branches shifted, but it was only the wind. The broken slab of the outside shower loomed like a tombstone. A large lizard on the high, bulky mass of the old water reservoir flicked its tail and disappeared into the shadows.

Occasionally they paused to shout, feeling a little foolish. They heard only the waves' thunk and woosh, sounding like Fourth of July fireworks being launched. In the short quiet of the ocean's ebb, they strained to hear above the other noises of the tropical night.

As they neared the back of the house, they found a blanket, thrown in a heap, on it a dark patch of what looked like heavy, clotted blood. On the first white stair up to the veranda, there was a brown, dried stain.

"Manuel was wounded, but the killer thought he was dead and wrapped him in a blanket?" Sixto hazarded.

"Why carry him *to* the blanket, if the purpose was to prevent a trail?" Balthazar shone the flashlight's beam on up the stairs. "And there's certainly a trail." Walking on the edge of the wide steps, they followed the blood-stains around the veranda to the foot of the outside staircase leading to the second story. The splotches, sprinkled over a wider area, continued up these steps.

"Could be," Balthazar said, "that it's the woman's blood on the blanket. The killer abandoned the plan to wrap her up and just carried her to the beach. But Manuel could have been shot somewhere upstairs. The killer, thinking he's dead, goes off to dispose of Emily deDiego. But Manuel staggers down the stairs when the killer is gone, gets on his horse, and rides off for help."

"Why kill Manuel upstairs? Was he just going to leave the body there?"

"Maybe the guy was trying some kind of set-up to frame Manuel for the whole bodies-on-the-beach business. Or Manuel could even have been in on the plan from the beginning. He might not have wanted the Señora to return here after so many years. He's been here all his life, bothered by no one. Suppose she decided to fire him. So he's been helping out the guy who set up this scheme to grab all the land—throwing the bodies on the back of the horse and dropping them off. If she couldn't be bought out or frightened off, she could be killed and the investigation would be thrown off by this other stuff."

Balthazar was beginning to be enthusiastic about his explanation. "But imagine, Sixto, what happens when Emily agrees to give Manuel a plot of the land before signing the rest over to Serena. He's all set now. But what the killer really intended was to get rid of Manuel in the end, anyway. Manuel gets suspicious, follows the killer upstairs. . . ."

"But the second floor was not used," Sixto interrupted. "I do not see why anyone would be up there."

Balthazar thought briefly. "Hell, I don't either," he said irritatedly. "Let's go up and look."

They went up single file, walking on the far edge to avoid stepping in the stains. Just a few steps up, they both stopped abruptly, startled by the uneven clicking sounds. Someone wounded—and with a gun—Balthazar thought, hiding up there? He put his hand on Sixto's arm to restrain him, turned off his flashlight and crouching down, gun in hand, crept slowly up until he was eye-level with the floor of the balcony. Slowly he straightened, but the uneven moonlight that filtered through the trees revealed little. Most of the rooms that opened off the long corridor were doorless, but shrouded in the darkness of the overhanging third story.

The sudden sweep of air past his cheek and the loud click near his ear made his stomach jump with fear. Again, the flick of sound, something almost brushing his head. Then he could see one in the sky. "Only bats," he said shakily. He turned his light on, and the startled bats swooped away from its beam down the hallway or into the darkened rooms. Standing by the side of the doorway of each one, guns drawn, they checked the once-elegant chambers. Their lights flitted across the remnants of tarnished gold-leafed ceiling trim,

rotting parquet floors, littered with chunks of mildewed
plaster. Despite the cold clammy air, both men were
sweating. The rooms held nothing but bats and huge,
scuttling rats.

They went back to the staircase. The awful trail of
stains went to the right and to the landing up to the
third floor. Balthazar stepped back, and shone his light
all around. Large sections of the stair railing were missing, and at the top he could see that the concrete
balustrade that had formed the balcony of the top floor
had crumbled, too, leaving gaps of darkness. But the
stairs going straight up seemed solid. They, too, were
marked with blood.

"Look," he whispered, pointing to one smeared
stain. "That's a heelprint, coming down!"

They turned off their flashlights simultaneously.
Surely, Balthazar considered, somebody must be up
there, or at least a body. Why else would a bleeding
man have dragged himself there? He must have been
patiently and painfully stalking someone up these stairs.
He called out again. The tall pines, arching above,
creaked and sighed, but there was no other sound.

He edged up the staircase, pausing at eyelevel.
Here the moonlight was brighter, but rubble was scattered about in piles everywhere. A man could easily be
stretched out behind one, perhaps injured, certainly
dangerous. Nothing moved. He flashed the light and
stepped forward carefully.

There was an occasional splotch of blood near the
remains of the railing, and a larger pool further on, not
far from the northeast corner. Then no more. Manuel
had stood there and then returned. Balthazar picked his
way to the very edge of the east side of the house. Here
the entire railing was missing, except for a few broken
ruins.

He shone his light down over the edge. Directly
below him was the huge water cistern, reaching almost
to the second story, its rotting wooden cover in place.
To the right was a towering banyan tree. He swung the
beam amid its exposed roots and around the rusted sides

of the enormous cistern, then he walked back to where Sixto was standing, shining his light down into the yard on the north where the blanket lay.

"You'd have to be a hell of a sentimentalist," Balthazar said sourly, "to climb up here just for a last dying look at the view."

"*Sí*, and then imagine the man dragging himself back down, jumping on a horse, and riding for help." They were silent a moment, remembering Manuel's destroyed face.

"That's a point, though. Where does he go after he comes down? The blood on the staircase was smeared, but not that on the back veranda."

At the base of the staircase, the trail of blood across the front grounds was nearly impossible to trace in the leaves. But at last they found a larger pool near the cistern.

"He probably leaned against this to rest," Balthazar theorized. "Watch out for that long cover handle here, Sixto. It sticks right out."

Sixto leaned against the concrete base of the cistern himself.

"Then," Balthazar went on, "he goes for the horse." He shone the light carefully around the area. "We're right. . . . Horses' hooves. It's Manuel we've been tracking. But damn," he raised his fist and thumped it against the surface of the water tank, setting off a hollow boom, "why did he go up—"

"*Baltasar*," Sixto said slowly, "*that's* the noise I heard."

"What noise?"

"This one." Sixto thumped the tank quickly several times. "Like someone hitting metal, but more . . . more . . . not so close."

Balthazar's light swung around the exterior of the house and through the grounds. "This is the only metal around."

"If someone were inside this," Sixto went on, "it would sound . . . ."

"Crawled in to hide, you mean? But you can only shut this lid from the outside, even if it still opens. . . ."

But Sixto was laboriously cranking the handle, and the huge lid of the tank shifted slowly outward. Balthazar clambered up the short ladder on the base, and then scrambled awkwardly up the tank's side, grasping a metal handhold near the top. Sixto handed up the flashlight.

Floating on the surface, face down, was the body of a man.

23

"VICTOR MALEN," Terron said, looking down at the sodden corpse. "Can't imagine it. Part of the town."

The jeep had been pulled back; the chain and hook of the front-end winch that had dragged the body out still dangled in front of the windshield. The young patrolman who had tried so long to revive Malen sat, his back against the tree, his shoulders slumped in defeat, his breath rasping in the silence. The portable floodlights both illuminated and eerily distorted the scene.

They cast queer shadows on the dead man's face, creating a parody of a devil's mask. The thick, tufted eyebrows stood up as if they were brushed, making the sunken eyesockets look even hollower, more like holes. The nose appeared huge, spread out across the cheeks. The shriveled mouth gaped open, the glitter of two gold-rimmed teeth caught the light.

"Had plenty of money," Terron observed shortly. Pulling up a bent garden chair with sagging webbing next to Balthazar's equally decrepit one, he tested the seat and slumped down. Perched on a teetering kitchen stool across from them, Sixto was glaring at the departing back of the medical examiner who had insisted the young agent report forthwith to the Emergency Room in Carolina for X-rays. Terron blew out his lips. "Would have thought he'd be satisfied. Could have bought a *lot* of land."

"I imagine," Balthazar said, slapping at the mosquitoes attracted by the bright lights, "that Malen knew that its real value lay in owning it *all*. And unless these old people could be frightened off the land, moved of their own accord, so to speak, he'd have a legal nightmare. They and the original owners would have to agree on price and compensation. But if most of the squatters moved out before he tried to buy it up, it'd be a lot easier. And, having all the land would give him absolute control."

"No such thing as too much money." Balthazar went on, trying to ignore his complaining stomach. It was almost eleven o'clock and he was thinking wistfully of what remained of Señora Cardenas' bounty back at the vacation center. "Malen probably never forgot how it felt to be a poor Puerto Rican busboy in New York."

"Can imagine *that*." Terron sighed heavily. "And you're pretty sure he *fell* in?"

"The bloodstains indicate Manuel was standing too far back to have pushed him. I think Malen intended to put *Manuel's* body in the cistern. He had Manuel all wrapped in a blanket. He opens up the tank down here, and he goes up to see if it's possible to get the body in the tank from above. Without help, he couldn't lift it—top of the tank has to be fifteen feet off the ground. They must have built them high in those days so there could be water pressure on the second story. But the angle's all wrong from that level, so he goes to the third."

"If Malen had managed it, and then closed the cover, don't know that we'd ever have looked in the thing. Looks like the top is rusted shut. He could have even broken the handle off."

"But Manuel wasn't dead," Balthazar pointed out. "Malen was used to shooting dead men, not live ones. He aimed carelessly."

Terron glanced up at the high roof. "He thinks Manuel is dead. Malen's up there right on the edge, looking down. He turns around and there's Manuel standing there, all quiet in the moonlight. Give you a turn."

Sixto grimaced. "A real *zombi*."

"It would be a shock," Balthazar agreed quietly, "particularly given Malen's mental state. All it'd take was one unthinking step backwards."

The three men looked up at the moldering edge of the balcony, where the bats now circled and swooped, feasting on the unexpected bonanza of insects. Balthazar shook his head. "Perhaps Malen never intended to kill anyone. He'd been planning this a long time, quietly buying up pieces of land, figuring out how to get rid of the remaining squatters. Wait a minute, what was his eventual plan there? He panics the people into wanting to move, but they couldn't afford it."

He snapped his fingers. "How about this? He goes to Mayor Couvertier and suggests moving all those frightened old people into the blocks of tidy little unsold houses in town. Generous Señor Malen will buy some from the city at their absolute cost, the people have their government checks and can pay a low rent. Both the mayor and Malen will look good, and it would cost Malen much less in the long run."

Terron rubbed his drooping eyelid. "Makes you wonder—the way things turn out. You know those people would have liked that—nice new houses, neighbors. But if Malen had brought it up in any sensible way, without public pressure, the mayor would have said, 'No, the houses are for all the people who will move here when the bridge is finished.' And some of the old people wouldn't want to move. And there'd be a lot of fuss, and nothing done."

He stopped, picking at the threads of webbing on the arm of the chair. "Always happens that way here. In my own case, well, didn't want to go into it with you, thought you'd be sure it had something to do with the bodies. But see, what we need here is a *balneario*. People'd like a public beach with showers, room to park. Nearest one is all the way into Isla Verde. And my mother owned a little piece next to the best road. She liked it out there—and I could stop in most days. Couldn't imagine anyone buying it. But then when she took so sick, I started thinking—the government might take it. Wouldn't get much, but something."

He put his solid forearms on his thighs and gazed stonily at the ground. "But politics in this town! I was afraid that the mayor'd think of it, too. And he'd stick the *balneario* wherever people who'd help his career wanted it. Could be miles from a decent road—just like his pavilion. But, if I told you, you'd have to check it out. Then there'd be no way to keep it quiet. Anyway, that's how Panama and me figured it. Couvertier was set to run for a county office; we thought we'd wait for a new man."

He looked up at the detectives guiltily. "Should have told you, though. It'd have got you thinking the right way, maybe, even though there was so little money involved—a few thousand—that I couldn't see. . . . Damn! Checked the property-tax records myself, like I said, to see if my mother'd paid up.· She had. But I never thought to look at the other old folks' records to see if they actually owned their land like my mother did. Sorry," he concluded gruffly.

"But, as you say," Balthazar put in tactfully, "there wasn't enough money in a government condemnation of a portion of the land to justify what was occurring. And a few of the old squatters would have gotten something out of that, just as you would have. They would have been satisfied, perhaps. What baffled all of us was that the motive was the necessity to acquire *all* the land, and the fact that it couldn't simply be *bought* by somebody with enough money. The original owners might be happy to sell, but if some of the squatters refused to move, there'd be a lifetime of court cases."

"Think Malen had always planned to get the deDiego land himself?" Terron asked.

"He probably didn't think there was any need to hurry. He was prepared to outwait the old woman. If she died without a will, which was probable given her condition, there'd be a public auction. If not, her heirs would probably be happy to sell.

"But everything went sour for Malen in a hurry.

Probably the president of the country club called up this afternoon all excited by Serena Burns's offer. Malen was no doubt a major stockholder, but if her offer was pretty high, he'd have a hard time convincing the others not to sell. And then he's told she's also planning to acquire the deDiego land."

He swatted a particularly foolhardy mosquito on his forearm. "That has to be very bad news for him. If, as we suspect, he'd been patiently buying up other land in the area under the names of dummy corporations, he'd have quite an investment in land. It could now be worthless. Serena, or any other possible buyer, would have trouble getting the intervening pieces from the squatters. There'd be no market for his scattered pieces. But, if he could get rid of Emily deDiego before she signed anything, Serena might lose interest, go elsewhere. Señora deDiego was going to *donate* her land to the religious community, not sell it. With Emily dead, Serena would have to buy it, and she might be faced with a drawn-out probate case at that. Malen had no time to plan. Tonight must have looked like the best time to act, since everybody's attention was on the Voodoo ceremony."

"If we'd found the Señora dead and Manuel gone," Terron mused, "wonder what I would have thought? Might have occurred to me that Manuel was in back of the whole thing. He always seemed a quiet-type person. He didn't mingle much. Nobody knew him very well. Lived out here all by himself. I'd probably have just been glad to get the whole thing over. And, come to think of it, a horse would be the easiest way to get the bodies on the beaches. Think he did that?"

"A donkey would be just as useful," Balthazar replied. "I think Albin was more likely the one who helped Malen dump the corpses. Albin was always wandering around the beach at night. Anybody who saw him wouldn't give it a second thought. He was part of the landscape. Malen was safe in hiring him, too. No matter what Albin said, would you have believed him?"

"No, no," Terron shook his head. "Suppose he'd

even come right into the station and told me he did it. So I say to him, 'Why?' He says Señor Malen hired him, gave him some money for rum. I'd have given Albin a cup of coffee and sent him on his way. I'd probably have told him to watch his mouth. But maybe Malen thought you two would be more likely to listen to the old man, being outsiders and all. Smarter just to get rid of Albin. Probably thought we'd never question the accident. And we didn't." He winced bitterly.

"A man with the reputation of a public benefactor." Balthazar said thoughtfully. "His partner Fred McMurdie said he had a reputation for helping out their employees over in Haiti. Small sums for weddings, help them arrange funerals. That might have even involved arranging bodies to be shipped for burial elsewhere, maybe to the other side of the island, to the Dominican Republic. Maybe the coffins came here instead. I wonder. If you showed photographs of those corpses you found to McMurdie, think he'd recognize any of their workers?"

"We can try it, but I got a feeling that Malen would have chosen their relatives, rather than the workers themselves. Could even have paid for paupers' funerals," Terron observed. "He was a smart man. Close, too. His name never showed up in connection with any of the corporations that owned land around here. 'Course, I wouldn't have thought anything about it if it did."

"He was cautious. Even McMurdie didn't think his partner had large real estate investments. Malen must have been really surprised to walk into the restaurant the day after we arrived and hear us asking questions about local land ownership."

"Hmm. Think he was upset enough to run you down with a bus?'

"Look at it this way. A few months back you asked to look at the tax records. Some clerk maybe mentions that. But Malen's been pretty careful to buy land through private companies. And nothing further is said. He thinks the whole matter is forgotten. But that morning, the mayor of Rio Grande calls him over and introduces him to us as a man who knows all about real estate. Now Montanez probably said that innocently. What he meant was that Malen was a sharp businessman, that he would know a lot about such things. In any case, we'd been discussing a whole range of possibilities. But Malen doesn't know that. He doesn't want a full-scale investigation. It could have worried him enough to take some action. And since he knew McMurdie well, he surely would be able to guess we'd be out at the country club that day for a long, long time. He had plenty of time to set up his plans. All he had to do was wait for us in the school bus."

Balthazar turned to Sixto. "Not," he said, "that I think Malen was in back of trying to snare us with a fishing line. That sounds more like Albin was doing a little panicking on his own."

"Sí," said Sixto, grinning. Far from looking like a man drowsy from a possible concussion, the young detective seemed more alert, Balthazar thought, than Terron appeared or he himself felt. "The old man sees us beating up on the big man with the machete at the *Restaurante*. Thinks we're tough guys from San Juan and becomes scared that it won't take us too long to find out all about what he's done." Sixto started to shake his head, but then thought better of it.

"Fishing line?" Terron asked. He looked from Balthazar to Sixto. "What are you talking about? You didn't mention any problem."

"Well," Balthazar replied wearily, "we couldn't prove anything. We come in two days in a row and tell you that we've been attacked. What would you have thought?"

"I'd have told you that you were in Loiza, not San Juan," Terron admitted reluctantly. "I'd have said things are quieter out here. We still got a nice mess, though. Theorizing's fine. Smart of you to figure this out," he admitted with grudging admiration. "But we can't prove much. Manuel's dead, you know. And the Haitian witch doctor just keeps telling the drummer to tell us that the spirits spoke, not him. Claims he himself doesn't speak a word of Spanish. No, no. But he did get a very queer look on his face when I shouted that if he didn't answer my questions, I'd dump him in the big jail in San Juan."

"If Malen were alive, the *hougan* would keep insisting the spirits spoke, I'm sure. Malen probably promised him a round sum when he got home to Haiti. Show him Malen's body, he'll probably talk. After all, even if he admits to telling stories, what would we charge him with? Impersonating a snake? Giving inaccurate weather forecasts? But his evidence will be useful. And when Malen's will is probated, his holdings will be public. We can make a reasonable case for our reconstruction of events."

"Too bad," Terron looked pityingly at the sheeted body. "Still, you know, if he'd lived, I'm not sure we could have gotten Malen on anything. What's more, if he came up with any kind of a plausible story about what happened here, I'd have believed him. Suppose he'd said he was driving by, heard this noise, found Manuel had killed the Señora, struggled for the gun. Who knows? We might even have thrown Manuel in jail for Señora deDiego's murder."

"Possible, isn't it?" Balthazar got up gingerly, but found to his surprise that his knee was only a little stiff. "The water *loa* got Malen after all. Felicity Sterling will appreciate that."

"Maybe," Terron added, "but Manuel closed the lid on the water cistern."

"If Malen had not put the Señora's body just there on the beach," Sixto said, with real uneasiness in his voice, "I would not have fallen. I would have figured out where the noise was coming from. He was pounding and pounding. He was drowning, and I did not realize."

"Not so sure he drowned," Terron said, eying the tank. "Cover looks pretty airtight. Metal seal around the wood— meant to keep out insects, sand. He could have treaded water for a long time. Probably suffocated. Buried alive."

ABOUT THE AUTHOR

M. J. ADAMSON lives in Colorado and Puerto Rico.

☐ 25789-7 **JUST ANOTHER DAY IN PARADISE,**
Maxwell $2.95

Fiddler has more money than he knows what to do with, he's tried about everything he'd ever thought of trying and there's not much left that interests him. So, when his ex-wife's twin brother disappears, when the feds begin to investigate the high-tech computer company the twin owns, and when Fiddler finds himself holding an envelope of Russian-cut diamonds, he decides to get involved. Is his ex-wife's twin selling high-tech information to the Russians?

☐ 26201-7 **NOT TILL A HOT JANUARY,**
Adamson $2.95

Introducing New York Homicide Detective Balthazar Marten. Balthazar Marten finds himself on special assignment in San Juan, Puerto Rico, far from the cold New York streets. Things really heat up when three coeds are strangled and Marten finds himself on the trail of a psycho.

☐ 25717-X **THE BACK-DOOR MAN,** Kantner $2.95

Ben Perkins doesn't look for trouble, but he isn't the kind of guy who looks the other way when something comes along to spark his interest. In this case, it's a wealthy widow who's a victim of embezzlement and the gold American Express card she gives him for expenses. Ben thinks it should be fun; the other people after the missing money are out to change his mind.

☐ 26061-8 **"B" IS FOR BURGLAR,** Grafton $3.50

"Kinsey is a refreshing heroine."—*Washington Post Book World*

"Kinsey Millhone . . . is a stand-out specimen of the new female operatives." – *Philadelphia Inquirer*

[Millhone is] "a tough cookie with a soft center, a gregarious loner." —*Newsweek*

What appears to be a routine missing persons case for private detective Kinsey Millhone turns into a dark tangle of arson, theft and murder.

Look for them at your bookstore or use the coupon below: